LITTLE CRIMINALS
Death Before Dishonor

BY BELOVED S. ALLAH

Dorrance Publishing Co
585 Alpha Drive
Suite 103
Pittsburgh, PA 15238
Visit our website at *www.dorrancebookstore.com*

ISBN: 978-1-6491-3846-0
eISBN: 978-1-6491-3864-4

I dedicate this book to my children.

May you never have to live this life and know your father loves you, and to all of those who I knew and lost over the years who couldn't see just because it glitters doesn't mean it's gold and got caught up in the game.

Little Criminals

Death Before Dishonor

Koran was about 12 when he and his mother moved out to Queens. Koran wasn't a bad kid. Yet with no father around he was always running the streets. His grandmother, "Peaches," who raised him, thought now that his mother had herself together and wanted to be a mother, leaving Brooklyn and moving to Queens would be a good place for them to move, and for them to try and get to know each other. Koran's grandmother knew that if he stayed in Brooklyn, dead or in jail was how he would end up like a lot of other kids where they lived....

It was the summer of '85. Four friends—Lil' L, Koran, Randy, and Shawn—were just some young kids being teenagers. Little did any of them know that they would be going from being just kids who hung out together to well-known criminals.

It was the first day of school, and for some they just couldn't wait, yet for Koran it meant meeting new people who would be quick to want to know where he lived, what was his name, why did he leave Brooklyn to move to "Rosedale Queens," and a lot of other questions he did not want to answer. Koran was standing at the bus stop waiting for the bus to take him to school, when a guy who he had seen a few times said to him, "What's up, kid? My name is Randy, what's yours?"

"I'm Koran," he answered with some hesitance.

Randy was son of a preacher who tried to run with the wrong crowd every chance he got—a true mama's boy.

No sooner than he stepped off the bus, Koran was confronted with one of those moments where he wished he was somewhere else. He and Randy got confronted by Lil' L and Shawn, who were neighborhood troublemakers and small-time criminals.

"So who the fuck is ya friend, Randy?" Shawn asked.

Koran looked at Shawn and Lil' L hard, staring them in their eyes, and said, "The name is Koran! You have a problem with that, we can deal with it right now!"

Lil' L had been in and out of youth homes for just about everything, from pushing weed to stealing cars. He had just done six months for being in a stolen car with his brother, who was killed by the police.

Shawn was a wannabe thug, AKA drug dealer, who was the younger brother of Brian, who wanted nothing more than to be like the big drug dealers out in Queens who had young guys selling weed in 231 Park and crack on 228th Street. Koran stood there, still staring them down, waiting for the moment when he would have to fight for having done nothing more than stepped off a bus.

Things got heated for a minute, then Lil' L yelled, "Yo, cut the bullshit! We have shit to do!"

They hit the corner store, got a few bags of chips, a few 40-s, and a couple White Owls. Lil' L told everybody to meet up after homeroom so they could go crash at one of his girlfriends' houses and smoke this weed he had.

Koran wondered, *How are we supposed to do this?*

Randy seemed to be reading his mind. "Yo, man," Randy told Koran, "don't sweat it. All you need to do is get signed into your homeroom and we'll be back before school is out."

Koran thought to himself that things out in Queens might not be that bad. It was not Brooklyn, but he was willing to give it a try.

As the bell rang, Lil' L said, "So I'll be right over here, you niggers go ahead to school," as he reached in his pocket and pulled out a bag of weed.

It was now 9 A.M. As they all snuck out of school, Koran, Randy, and Shawn were all looking for Lil' L, who was outside in the back of the school smoking a blunt.

Shawn said to Koran, "So, nigger, you ready to get paid? Shit, I thought all you niggers from Crooklyn… I mean Brooklyn, knew how to steal."

Koran took two hits on the blunt and passed it to Randy, and before Randy could take a hit Koran punched Shawn in the mouth.

Lil' L stepped in between them and said to Koran, "I see you're kind of nice with ya hands, so what about BNE's?" Lil' L paused as if he was sizing Koran up. "If you're game," he told them, "let's go, for I know the perfect house, if not take ya ass back to school."

Koran's head was spinning from the weed and the adrenaline. He thought to himself, *Now what do I do? Go back to school and get called a punk? Or ride with the only friends I've met?*

His thoughts were interrupted by Randy's voice. "Yo, yo, the bus!"

In that split second, Koran made his choice. They all got on the bus smelling like weed and alcohol. The bus stopped off of Farmers Blvd.

Lil' L said, "Yo, that's the house right there. Randy, check to see if anybody's home."

Shawn waited to kick the door in as Randy told him nobody was home.

Shawn looked at Koran and said, "Your bitchass thinks you're one of us now!" and kicked the door open.

As the door flew open, one by one they all ran in the house.

Lil' L yelled, "Everybody hit a room and let's get the fuck out of here!"

A few days later, Koran found out that the house they robbed was the house of one of Randy's friends, some chick named Marry Ann, whom Lil' L had him talk to so they could find out what she had worth taking. For the next couple of days, the four of them hit damn near every house in Rosedale, always taking the stuff to a pawn shop on Hillside Ave. and splitting the money. Koran's grandmother and mother had no idea that Koran would leave Brooklyn only to move to Queens to become a person that broke in people's homes, sometimes doing two, three homes a day, yet for Koran and his friends it was something that made them a family, and for anyone who fucked with them meant fucking with all four.

In between dipping out of school to rob houses or going up to other schools to start fights, they would ride the bus or train, pickpocketing people. This was where Lil' L came to learn not only was Koran like that with his hands, he was also the best pick pocket out of all of them.

One day before they cut school to rob a house, Koran asked Randy, "Why do you change clothes every day when you come to school?"

Randy looked embarrassed at first, but then answered, "Yo, man, my mom and dad can't afford the stuff a lot of kids in school have, plus I have two other brothers who need stuff, so I steal so I'm able to get the stuff I want without asking my parents. I leave it in my locker at school so they won't find out." Randy looked at Koran and felt like he could trust him. He continued. "I never had any real friends, and I guess you guys are it?"

Koran looked at the ground for a long time, then said, "Man, at least you have both parents.... I don't know, my father and my mom was hardly home because she was always out laying up with some nigger, so it's like I don't know her either. Even though what we do is wrong, you guys are all I have and I just want more than the little I have now. I always wear my cousin's stuff that he doesn't want anymore. I want my own."

Randy nodded, signaling that he understood, and said to Koran, "Yo, man, you know why Shawn is always talking' shit to you? Because man, before you started kicking it with us Lil' L was always with him. Now Shawn feels like you two are closer than they were. Oh, and also, man, he thinks you're a 'pretty' motherfucker."

Koran looked at Randy with a puzzled look on his face. "A pretty motherfucker! What the hell is that?"

"I'm just saying," Randy continued, "you may not have much, but looking at you people would think you got it going on, plus, nigger, you never like getting dirty."

Koran looked at his friend with half a smile. "Man, I'm just trying to come up." Koran told Randy, "I come from a home where there was always at least five people there, and if I wasn't fighting one of them for shit to eat, then it was the roaches and rats that ran around.... I'm just trying not to live like that."

Koran and Randy were standing outside Springfield HS, and they saw Shawn and Lil' L coming towards them. As they got closer, they noticed Shawn had a busted lip.

"Yo, man, what happen to you?" Randy asked.

"Nothing," Shawn replied quickly. "Me and my older brother just got into it over a bag a of weed."

Lil' L interrupted and Shawn seemed relieved that the spotlight was no longer on him. "So where y'all little criminals want to go get paid today?" Lil L continued without waiting for their response. "What Koran says? Little Criminals, you know, L.C. Crew, I heard some old man talking on the corner of 147th and 231st, saying, 'Yeah, these damn little criminals have broke into my house too,' shit, not knowing I was one of the people he was talking about. He was like 'Yeah, they even eat my damn food and ran up my phone bill.' Okay, cool, so the L.C. Crew is who we are."

The others nodded in agreement.

"Yeah," Randy said, "L.C. Crew...."

L.C. Crew, L.C. Crew, L.C. Crew, before you knew it any and everybody they knew was calling them that. If you wanted weed you went to Shawn, you wanted a car or some crazy shit like that you went to Lil' L, you wanted a credit card, bus pass/train pass, you spoke to Koran, and if you wanted something done that you didn't want to do there was Randy, willing to do it as long, as there was food he was down with it. But if somebody wanted a person's house robbed or something at a cheaper price than what was in the store, you spoke to Little Criminals.

It was about 11:30 on a Thursday night, and Koran got a knock on his door. It was Lil' L.

"Yo, what's up, man, I need to stay here the night, I can't go home. My dad is trippen', plus the school called again, telling him I haven't been there in about two months."

"Damn, man, do you know what time it is?" Koran saw that his family was not the only one that was fucked up and yelled, "Go upstairs, man! Do you want something to eat or anything before I go to bed?"

Lil' L answered, "I'm good, man."

Here was where the friendship between Koran and Lil' L changed to where not only did they start dressing alike, they started calling each other cousins.

Friday morning, it was another day of cutting school, breaking into a few homes, and smoking weed.

Lil' L said, "Yo, let's go hit some of those houses over by the Long Island railroad."

Everybody gave the sign that they were all cool with it as they jumped on the Q5 bus that would drop them off right up the street from where they were going.

Koran told Lil' L, "Nigger, we never been here before, nor do we know over here, if some shit breaks out then what?"

Lil' L said, "Look, man, if something happens everybody just cross the tracks and we'll met up at Mentone Park."

Randy hit the door. He had been given the name "Batman" because of the way he looked in the big coat his mom made him wear.

As they all rushed the house, Lil' L was in one bedroom, Koran in the master bedroom, and Randy was in another, helping Shawn put stuff in their bookbags.

Lil' L walked in the hallway and asked Shawn, "Do you hear something?"

Shawn replied, "That's not me, it's the owner of the house."

The man yelled out, "Okay, motherfucker, if you're not out my house by the time I count to three, I'm going to kill ya ass."

By the time he got to two, he cocked his gun and headed for the stairs. Koran jumped through the window, cutting his right arm, and Lil' L jumped through another as Shawn waited to see where he was going. Randy hid in the closet until he thought it was safe, then ran out, almost getting shot. Times passed as everyone made it out safe with just Koran and Lil' L both getting cuts on their arms, standing in Mentone Park, hiding, looking to see if the police were on the way.

Shawn said, "I thought you Brooklyn niggers were smarter than that."

Koran said to Shawn, "I take it you want me to whip ya ass a second time? I told, I told ya ass not to hit that house!" Koran yelled at Lil' L.

"Nigger, did you see all the shit he had in that house?"

"Look, motherfucker, do it look like I'm smoken'? I'm not going up in another house without me knowing nobody is home. Give me some time to come up with something," said Koran, "but in the meantime, we need to get the fuck from around here."

"Let's go to Green Acres," said Shawn.

"Cool," said Randy, "because I'm hungry."

"Fuck the food, man, I need another Adidas jacket, plus we can catch a flick until it's cool to go home."

Lil' L liked that idea and everybody caught the bus to the mall. All the way there Koran was wondering how did that man creep up on them like that, then he remembered seeing something about an alarm.

A few weeks passed and everybody was at Koran's house with a few girls that cut school with them, drinking and smoking weed.

Koran told the guys, "After these girls help clean my house and leave, I want to show you something."

They each went into a room and did their thing. A few hours passed and it was time to get down to business.

"So what you wanted to talk about, Randy?" as he lit a blunt.

"That shit that almost got us killed two weeks ago is what! I got a book on alarms that teaches how to disconnect alarms. I also got us a few radios from Radio Shack. This way we can talk to each other when we're in the house. After the alarm is cut and if some shit jumps off, we'll have the heads-up."

"Yo, it sounds like a plan," said Lil' L. "Now let's go to McDonald's, for a nigger is starving, plus ain't shit here to eat."

"That's fucked up, man, how they kicked you out of our school," Koran said to Randy.

"I know, man, I was liking it there too, had some nice little females in there, but the ones at IS.59 are much better than them females at 231. There's this one girl kid and damn, anyway, let's go eat."

"Nigger, nobody told you to go to school with a gun that was a lighter."

"If I can recall, mother fucker, the gun lighter your ass is talking about I got from you, Shawn! I didn't hear you saying shit when we were in school together sticken' niggers up in the bathroom."

"No, ya didn't, nigger, shit, I was getting that money!"

"No, I was getting that money," said Koran, "you were just there watching the door."

"The both of you need Jesus in ya life," said Randy. "Yo, look, Batman, going to church may work for you yet, praying to a mystery God don't feed me. I see you been readying some more of that shit ya uncle or cousin Sha King has been giving you to read, Koran. You know it wouldn't hurt if you niggers picked up a book ever now and then. I'm out, man, I get with y'all later."

"Randy, I'll be at Kathy's house if you need me."

Lil' L leaned over to Shawn and said, "Damn, that nigger is over there every day, she must be giving him some ass."

"Yo, I heard that! Kathy is like my older sister, plus the cool shit is she lives right next door to me. She schools me on the shit girls do and stay with a gang of bad females. I play my cards right, I can hit all her friends and you'll be sitting here playing with ya dick looking at Shawn."

The next day Koran ran into Shawn waiting for the bus.

"So nigger, where they hell you're going?" said Shawn.

"I'm about to catch the 113 bus so I can go to the flea market out in Far Rock."

"Flea market?" said Shawn.

"Yes, nigger, are you deaf? I need to go cop some Pumas so I can wear them to a party over in Rochdale tonight."

"Why not go on the Ave.? If ya ass was going on the Ave. I'd give you a ride."

"I'm good. we on the Ave. damn near everyday. My sister told me about this spot so that's where I'm going."

"I don't know why you spend so much time over that bitch house if you ain't getting the pussy."

"Shawn, look," said Koran, "I'm not too far from kicking your ass as it is now, so why don't you just get the fuck out of here! My sister name is Kathy… . Bitch is what your mama is!"

Beep, beep, beep.

"Yeah, nigger, go run to ya mother, she's probable paging you to tell you she needs more condoms," Korans said, laughing as he ran for the bus.

Later on that night, Shawn and Lil' L came over to Koran's house.

"Come on, nigger, let's go!"

"I coming! I coming!"

"Damn, what took you so long?"

"I had to find which jean suit I wanted to wear."

"Yo, that was your mom who let us in?" said Lil' L.

"Yeah, nigger, and before you say something fucked up keep it to yourself."

"I was just going to say ya mom has it going on."

"Look, motherfucker, don't talk about my mother, I get enough of that bullshit from niggers in the street. That nigger in her room probable don't even know I'm her son, you know like I do she probable said I'm her little brother or something."

"Yo, we need to go get Randy!" said Koran.

"Nigger, please, you know his ass is not going to a party in Rochdale; his mom probable has him copying the Bible or some crazy shit."

"So it's just us three niggers," said Shawn.

"Fuck it, three it is," said Koran.

"Yo, we need to stop at the store so I can pick up some Newports and a White Owl."

"So who has the weed?" Koran asked.

"Nigger, ya know I do," said Shawn.

Just then Lil' L turned up the car stereo. "You know that's the shit, Fat Fat Boys! Yo, kid, get me a Sun dew juice and a bag of Boonton's, Koran!"

"Damn, man, every time I go to the store you got ya hand out, all these fucken' houses we rob you never got money, Shawn."

"Stop acting like a bitch and just look out for a nigger, damn, Koran."

"Nigger, I got you. So where the hell is this party at?"

"Shawn, just drive!" yelled Lil' L and Koran.

"That's it over there, where the music is playin'," said Koran.

"Okay, now look, we're going to go up and here, speak to a few of the bitches and see if we can line up some work for next week," said Shawn.

"Nigger, I don't recall you being my mother or father," said Koran.

"Cut the shit!" Lil' L said. "Damn, do y'all like each other or something? Every day the two of you beef over some bullshit. Oh, and as for us going up in here to see if we can line up something for next week, not here, nigger. Look around, that's the 113 percent over there, plus these are apartment buildings, only, what, two ways in the building, one way in the apartment. Some shit goes wrong, what we going to run across the roof?"

"Shawn, look up there, that shit is more than ten floors. We're here for one thing, pussy, nothing else; if we can come off with a number or two to some bitches that live over by us, then cool."

Eight blunts later and about six 40s, Lil' L, Shawn, and Koran headed back to Rosedale.

"Yo, I've been looking at this spot on Hillside, it's not a house, it's a corner where we can pump weed from," said Lil' L.

"So you want to say weed, man?" said Koran.

"It's good money in that shit," Shawn said, "just think, we could catch all the white boys up there and bag some pussy along the way."

"I'm game, man, but when will I go to school if I'm doing this plus B.N.E.s?"

"Yo, look, it's just a thought. I know some people I can get some weed from."

"Sorry, Shawn, can't fuck with ya, brother. That nigger be on some grimy shit," said Lil' L.

"Nigger, stop acting like you don't know what he's talking about!" said Koran. "I remember ya brother kicking your ass over a bag of weed back in the days, nothing personal. If the nigger was to ever try to beat us out our money, you know the rest of that story."

"You and Lil' L are the ones who don't seem to mind being all in the limelight. As for me, I'll play the sideline any day."

"Nigger, please, there's no money like new money," said Lil' L.

"True," said Shawn, "this nigger don't know!"

"What I know is all things come to an end, shit, what's wrong with slow money? It give ya ass a chance to enjoy it more."

"Yo, drop me off here," Shawn said to Lil' L. "I'll get with ya niggers tomorrow."

"So what you about to get into, Koran?"

"Nigger, I'm about to fall out, you just make sure you put ya dad shit back before he gets up for work."

"FUCK YOU!" yelled Lil' L.

"Come on, man, my neighbors are sleeping. Yo, swing by in the morning so you can drop me off at school!"

"School!"

"Yes, nigger, school, ya know, that place where you never go."

"Yo, L, for real, man!"

"Koran, what's this letter I got in the mail saying you haven't been in school? Your ass is going to be just like your no-good-ass father, keep fucken' up!"

"Boy, you need to listen to your mother when she's talken' to you," said Koran's mother's new boyfriend.

"Who the fuck is you! You're just some nigger who's fucken' my mother."

Before Koran could make it to his room, his mother had smacked him in the face.

"What the fuck are you looken' at?" Said Koran to his mother's boyfriend. "The only reason I'm even here is because of my grandmother, you don't give a fuck about me, all of a sudden you want to be my mother!"

Just then the doorbell rang and it was Lil' L."

Koran ran out the house as his mother yelled, "You better have you ass in school when I come up there today."

"Damn, man, what happen to you? Ya moms was in there kicking ya ass?"

"Yo, stop the fucken' car! I'll take the bus."

"Nigger, you think you're the first person who mom or dad be kicken' their ass?" said Lil' L. "Shit! My dad comes home and gets to drinking, he beats on me and my mother."

It was now 9:30, and Koran and his mother were in the principal's office.

"Well, Ms. Biggs, I'll get to the point. Your son has been getting into fights every other day. Most of his classes he's not attending; however, he does well on most of the tests he shows up for. Is there anything going on at home? Is his father in his life?"

"Things at home are fine. Look, I'm a single parent doing the best I can for Koran."

"Please understand, Ms. Biggs, I'm not trying to come down on you," said the principal. "I'm just trying to get to the reason your son is behaving the way he is. Do you know a few days ago your son told a teacher who asked him to take his hat off, 'You didn't buy my fucken' hat, so go run that shit on somebody else'?"

"No, I didn't," said Koran's mother.

The bell rang and the principal let Koran go to class and Koran's mother left.

Later that night, Koran was in bed sleeping and his mother came in the room with a telephone cord and beat Koran until he was black and blue, then said that he was a no-good child and his black ass would be just like his father.

Koran cried himself to sleep. Damn, time to get the fuck up for school. He looked in the mirror at all the marks on his body from the ass whippen' his mother put on him for having to come up there. A blue hoody and his hat down low to cover his face. For the next couple of weeks, Koran thought about killing his mother and himself, feeling like he had nothing to live for, so he went to see his grandmother, "Peaches," who had always been a person who made him feel happy. It was his grandmother who helped raise him when his mother was running around in the streets getting high.

"So how have you been?" said Koran's grandmother, Peaches.

"I'm okay, Peaches, I'd like it better if I was living back here in Brooklyn with you."

"Well, that's nice," said his grandmother, "but you know a son needs to be with his mother, now when you get older you can live anywhere you want. Is your mama still on that shit? Your mother was only fifteen when she had you, and God knows there have been times I wanted to kill her for all the dumb shit she was doing. She wanted the street and the street is what I gave her. She left you here and we all tried the best we could in raising you. I know you two really don't know each other but try to work it out, will you do that for me?" Peaches said to Koran.

Koran told her that he would, but in his heart he knew he was not telling the truth, just like he knew she was still getting high and still having different men in and out of the house. Koran never did tell anyone about the things she would do to him or the dreams he would have. He just knew when he saved enough money and was old enough, he would be leaving home and cutting her out his life for good.

"Damn, did ya see Randy tonight? Wearing a fuckin' sky blue suit and those fucked-up shoes?" said Lil' L, "Yo, Koran, I know that's ya boy but damn, who picked that suit out? Yo, Koran, why you're not going to the dance?"

"Nigger, I'm not going for the same reason you two ain't going, shit! I can't go. The school told my mom I did something and said they would just mail my shit, so what high school are y'all going to?" said Koran.

"Spring Field Gardens," said Shawn.

"Shit, I can't believe your ass even graduated, Lil' L," said Koran.

"Yeah, junior high was the shit, now high school, no big thing, just more fucken' classes and more homework," said Lil' L to Shawn and Koran.

"Well, here's to getten' paid and bitches," said Shawn, then he took a swig of his 40-oz and a hit of the blunt he got from Lil' L.

Okay, first day of high school and everybody had their new shell-toed Adidas and Pumas, the older guys wore Bally shoes and all the little honeys were wearing name earrings and belt buckles with their name. Standing on the corner of Spring Field Gardens HS were Shawn, Lil' L, pretty Koran, and Randy looking like he was on his way to church.

"Damn, man, you should have put on what I gave you," said Koran.

Randy said, "Yo, man, I was trying to leave out before my mom got up, but my little brother started school today and just when I was about to bounce, she said she was going to drop me off at school."

"Yo, I know you're looking at all this pussy," said Lil' L.

"For it's like every other bitch out here, we're going to hit their house. Speaking of that, tell me what you think of this," said Koran. "Look, we all know how to run up in a crib and take shit, how about if I told all of y'all a better way to get the money and take our time?"

"Come on, nigger, speak!" said Lil' L.

"Look, you know how one of us be running game on a nigger as the other one be hitting their pockets, right? We need to do the same thing when it come to people houses we rob. Let me break it down, one of us will talk to a female or be up in some ass, another person takes her keys and makes a copy. Two, three days later, we just walk in the front door, take whatever we want, shit, lock the door when we leave and leave it up to them to figure out what the hell happen. We all know about going to the back of the house and hit the battery or sticking a gum wrapper to short out the alarm, this here is just another way of doing what we do. Oh, and check this out, and when there's a some nigger we get into or have beef with we take their wallet and leave it at the house we broke into so the police will be looking for him."

Lil' L said, "Nigger, I gots to give it to you, you're one quiet motherfucker, but when you say something it's a mouthful."

Shawn was so fucked up by what Koran just said, all he could say was "Nigger, about time you step up. Let me ask you something, nigger, how is it you know so much about doing B.N.E.s?" Shawn asked Koran.

"Shit, man, growing up with a mother who was never home and a father not in the picture, a nigger just learned that shit quick if ya want to eat, as soon as I save up enough money I'm out of here, and fuck my fucked-up family."

Shawn knew in his heart Koran was the one to set it off, even if Lil' L and him thought they were these real criminals like the guys they looked up to. At this time 231 Park was still making money yet, not only for weed, but for now crack was on the rise and Little Criminals were about to step up their game, just one thing, they would first have to take out the neighborhood drug dealer.

It was a lot of niggers out in Queens quick to give them a package, yet Little Criminals were not about to work for anybody. Little Criminals set out and did just like they talked about, setting up a weed gate on Hillside Ave., until Randy's mother one day came home and found a bookbag full of weed in Randy's room. Randy was never one not to do what his mother said, plus his father had no problem getting in that ass if he ever got out of line, so when Randy saw his mother standing in his room he came clean, telling his mother, "Oh, Koran and Lil' L told me to hold it."

Koran came home and saw Randy. "Yo, man, I need for you to tell Lil' L my mom founded the weed."

"It's cool, man."

"Also, I need for you to know," Randy said, "my mom and dad knows I got the bag from you."

"Damn, man, why did you tell her you got it from me? Shit!"

"She was too close to the pots and pans, plus she had the bag in her hand."

"Shit, man, we all know how ya mom is."

"I'm going to need for you to come with me tomorrow and do a house up the street where the twins live, so we can put that money back. That nigger Lil' L is talking about getting a half a key or a key and setting shop up in the park up the street. Brook Field Park can be a nice spot, a lot of niggers looking for shit, plus we can get all those white boys from off of 243rd."

"Man, my parents be in that park!" said Randy. "I can't fuck with that."

"I was just giving you the heads-up," said Koran. "Lil' L has some kind of idea to be the next Phat Cat or one of these other niggers out here flipping weight. Like I said before, I'm cool with just doing B.N.E.s and selling weed."

"Randy, I don't even know why you even do the shit you do with us, I mean, you have a mom and dad, everyone else in the crew family is fucked up so we became family."

Randy looked at Koran long and hard and said, "Yeah, I have both my parents but having a house full of little brothers shit gets tight, you feel me? Tired of my brothers wearing secondhand shit, you don't think I know people be laughing at me in school? But you, Koran, you always looked out for me and never made fun of me."

"I'm just being me, man, I know what it's like always wanting shit. I went to bed a lot of nights with nothing to eat because my mom and some nigger out getting high. But yo fucken' with weight will have the Feds and all kinds of motherfuckers up in your shit. Where are Shawn and Lil' L?"

"Not sure, I haven't seen them all day. Oh, nigger, who was that girl I seen you and Prince trying to get with?" said Randy,

"That's Shorty, remember, who I used to see in class when I was in IS.59?"

"Oh, what's that shit you used to call her? Oh, yeah, Sweet P. Always wondered what the hell that meant."

"Look, L, with an ass that fat the pussy could only be sweet."

"Ha, ha, ha, not funny, nigger, I ain't eating no pussy, Koran, but all jokes aside, she seems cool, kid, plus she's bad as hell."

"Yo, Randy, I bag that, I'm done fucken' with these other females."

"Nigger, you act as if you're getting married."

"I'm not saying all of that, Randy, I just think if I get with her she's the one to keep a nigger in line, plus she looks like she doesn't take any shit."

"You know what's so funny, every time we see each other in the hallway she always says, 'Hi, 59,' like she wants me to know who she is."

"Yo, Koran, go somewhere with all that mushy shit," said L.

"Damn, man, are you feeling okay? Ya ass sounds like you're in love."

"Randy, stop, player, I'm just say she is fine, plus pussy have never been a problem for me, shit, even my 3rd-period teacher is trying to give a nigger some ass."

"Okay, okay, I have to admit," said Lil' L as he rolled a blunt, "your teach got a fat ass, always calling you Beloved."

"Get the fuck out of here," said Randy. "Not the teacher, her assistant, you seen her, the one you were like damn and then walked into the lunchroom door. I got her number a few days ago, then Sweet P came into the picture so I kind of was holding off on speaking to one because a nigger is feeling them both."

"Yo, Randy, I'm thinking about moving out and just saying fuck it, get me a little basement apartment and do my thing. Shit, at home ain't getting no better. Mom still has niggers coming in and out of there, and the last two niggers looked a little older than me."

"God will figure something out for you, just allow Jesus."

"Come on with that shit, man, where is Jesus when I'm fighting my mother boyfriends or getting my ass kicked by my mom? Shit is crazy how I get more love from some niggers I rob with than in my own home. Yo, I'm out, I'm about to go grab something at McDonald's."

An hour later, Randy, Lil' L, and Shawn rolled up and everybody asked, "Where's the party at?"

Koran said, "Nigger, I don't know, your guess is better than mine."

Prince and Divine came in and said, "So you niggers ain't going to school today? If not Mia across the street is haven' a little party, we were on our way there."

"Who is going to be there?" asked Lil' L.

"Not sure," said Divine, "just know a lot of bitches."

Shawn, Randy, Koran, and Lil' L all realized this was a house that they hadn't robbed, so they all agreed to go. Not only were they about to hit this house, but the two houses next to it and across the street.

Prince knocked on the door. Mia came to the door and you could smell the weed and hear the music as one by one they all went into her house.

Lil' L looked at Shawn and told him, "This will be easy," and said to tell Randy and Koran to look around and meet him in the kitchen.

Ten or fifteen minutes passed and they all met in the kitchen.

"So what do you think?" Koran asked Lil' L.

"Mia has some shit we could pawn up in here, everybody just needs to find a girl, start talking to her, find out where they live and can hit they shit next week one by one."

Lil' L looked at Randy and said, "Yo, I'm about to take this hood rat in the bathroom and get my dick sucked. I need you to sneak out and go get that bitch Mia keys copied."

"Why me, nigger?"

"Because L says you're the only motherfucker that ain't getting no pussy right now. Plus, as it's so many niggers in here, her dumb ass probable won't even know we're the ones who took her shit."

"Good, because I never did like that bitch!" Shawn said.

"Nigger, he is just talking shit because she never gave him the pussy."

Lil' L, for some reason, enjoyed fucken' with Randy. "Yo, kid, that nigger played you."

Randy then said, "Shawn, shut the fuck up, nigger. Nigger, I got the pussy."

"Oh, shit!" laughed Koran. "This nigger did fuck that female, lucky motherfucker."

"Yo, Lil' L, what's up with the other houses across the street and next door?" said Koran.

"Nothing," said Lil' L. "What time is it?"

"9:40, nigger, look, tell the other two to not be all day with these bitches."

"I got you," said Koran, then left.

"It's now almost noon, how many of y'all got the address of one of these bitches in here and her keys made, because we need to hurry up and hit the house next door from here and across the street," said Lil' L.

Shawn spoke first and said, "I'm good on mine."

Randy said, "I have mine but I need to put her keys back. Just when this trick was given' me some pussy, this nigger Shawn walks in talking about he was looking for the bathroom."

"What about you, Koran?"

"Come on, man, money first, why you nigger were fucken' with these skinny-ass mud kickers I slid out and checked out the house across the street, then went upstairs with Mia older sister Debby and her girlfriend, plus got some ass."

"Nigger, stop lying," said Lil' L.

"Ask ya boy Shawn, he seen me come out her room."

"Nigger, they both still sleep upstairs. Ya fuck with these young-ass females, if you want give me an older female any day."

Koran told Randy, "Just go find the female and when you see her walk over to her, kiss her on the cheek, and say, 'I'll call you later,' and slip her her keys in her bag like I showed you. By any chance you fuck that up, just leave them in the bathroom."

Koran could see Lil' L was mad at the fact that Debby gave him the pussy and not him. Koran just said, "Come on, nigger, let's go get the money, we don't have that much time."

By 4 P.M. they had hit the other two houses on the block Mia lived on and was headed to Hillside Ave. so they could pawn all the shit they got.

"Yo, I have to go, man, I don't need my mom bitchen' and shit about me being late."

"It's cool, Koran, I'll drop your cut off on my way home."

Koran, Lil' L, and Shawn all headed to Hillside.

"You know I fucked Debby first?" said Lil' L.

"Nigger, if ya did ya did, I just know when I was up in it I didn't see your light-skin ass there, so I don't care about the shit you're talken'."

Lil' L and Koran got into it.

"NIGGER, WHAT THE FUCK IS YOUR PROBLEM!" said Koran. "If this is about some female, you're one weak motherfucker! Remember KDF? 'Keep Dollars Flowin',' remember that? Never put some ass before maken' money, nigger, you act like you all hard and shit, then act like this over some pussy. You want to know why Debby never gave you the pussy? Because you always tried to make your ass seem like you were better than anybody else, as if yo shit don't stink! Debby just wanted to be loved fucken', and Koran had no problem with that."

"Nigger, we fam and I got you, but don't trip because of some pussy."

"Yo, Lil' L, Koran is right, man," said Shawn. "I hate to say it, but the nigger is right."

"So you two niggers want to team up on me?" said Lil' L.

"Nigger, here you go," said Shawn. "Nigger, when you fucked Ivory did he act like that?"

"Wait, you fucked Ivory?" said Koran.

"Yeah, I fucked her! I fucked her a few times."

"Nigger, good for you then," said Koran.

"The pussy wasn't all that anyway, one is enough for me. I fucked her to just get the keys. You, on the other hand, was just on some sloppy-seconds shit."

Koran knew at this point even though they all were boys that at some point him and Lil' L would have a falling out, for if he could do some crab shit like fuck a girl he was talking to what else could he do, and for Shawn to know and not say shit it was probably a lot of other shit they both knew but didn't tell Koran or Randy.

Shawn said to Lil' L, "Damn, nigger, we came off with this one dude in the pawn shop, asked if we could get him some more jewelry." "Go in there and find out when does he want them," said Lil' L. "$3500 is a nice piece of change," Lil' L said to Koran.

"Yeah, it's okay, let me ask you something, when you hit the houses when we were all in Mia's house, how come you just didn't pocket some of that shit for ya self? The difference between me and some other niggers out there, Lil' L, is that these niggers don't know what it is to be loyal."

"And you do?" said Lil' L.

"The three of you are all I got, and you just don't fuck family, maybe you need to remember that," said Koran. "I'll with you nigger later," as he jumped in his cab.

"Where to?" said the cab driver.

"147 and 231st, and I'm going to need you to wait."

Koran pulled up by Randy's house, jumped the gate, and went to the back of the house. He counted 1, 2 , 3, 4, 5, 6 hundred and knocked on Randy's window.

"So how did shit go?" said Randy.

"Not bad, me and Lil' L got into it."

"Not over that Debby shit?"

"Come on, man, you don't remember when we all were slap boxing on the side of McDonald's and you did some fly shit and smacked the shit out of Lil' L like three times?"

"Man, that shit was like four months ago."

"Well, some people remember the smallest shit, anyway, I got a cab waiting."

"Randy, Mama wants you," said his little brother.

"Tell her I'm coming."

"Oh, yeah, nigger, that chick Sweet P lives off of Farmers with her grandmother, Divine from over that way was trying to kick it to her and got shut down."

"RANDY! Come here!" yelled his mother.

"Got a go, man, talk to you in school."

"So where to now?" said the cab driver.

"Yo, just drive! Drop me of by 228th, I can go for a turkey and cheese right about now."

Koran got out the cab and started to walk in the store when he saw two of his sister's friends, Michelle and Jackey.

"Hey, K," said the girls as they walked out the store, smiling and switching their big asses.

"Ya sister is in the store."

"K, I need some money for some weed," said Kathy.

"Damn, girl, all these nigger out here and you ask me."

"Yeah, motherfucker! I'm asking you because you're my brother, when you be coming to me about these stink lil' bitches do I act like that?"

"You right," Koran said and gave his sister $20.

Kathy snatched $50 and said, "You know I love you, come by later, got something to tell you."

"Yo, yo, let me get a turkey and cheese and a beef patty with a cocoa bread."

Beep, beep, beep.

"Who the hell is this?" said Koran. He picked up the payphone and called the number. "Somebody just paged me?"

"Yeah, this is Debby, if you ain't doing nothing come by and pick me up."

"Yo, give me about 45 minutes, I need to run home first."

"Yo, Koran, don't have me waiting all night, don't forget to bring some weeds! Plus I'm horny, use the back door, see you when you get here."

"Shit, that's what I'm talking about."

Koran walked up to the corner of the block and got a cab, asked for car #7, jumped in, and said, "Yo, take me home, man, and I'm a need for you to wait."

Koran got to his house and saw his mom home, and like always her and some nigger goin' at it. "No need for me sticken' my noise in their shit, for the last time I did that I ended up getting hit by her and them fools staying together."

Koran went in his room without speaken', closed his room door, then popped up the floorboard in his closet. He snatched the money he got from the houses he robbed earlier and placed the money in the hole in the floor, took a quick shower, then got dressed and went to see Debby. On the ride there, Koran was asking himself how long was this shit with him and Debby going to last, after all she was much older than him and he was not even out of high school.

Now Debby was a bad chick in her early thirties, back door open just like she said, music playin' and the lights turned down.

Koran stopped and said to himself, "If this fuckin' female is trying to set me up, I'm going to kill her and her skinny-ass sister."

Koran opened the bedroom door and found Debby lying across the bed with just a thong on.

Before Koran even got the ass, he asked her, "Why are you fucken' with me?"

Debby got up and said, "Because I like ya lil' fine ass, you're not like those niggers you hang with, you're different. I know I'm older than you, so what! As long as you treat me right and break me off the way you do, that's all that matters." Debby asked Koran, "What's that in the bag?"

He pulled out a bottle of Moët and told her, "Sorry, love, I don't do 40 ounces." He reached in his Adidas jacket and pulled out a fat bag of weed.

It was a little after 12 A.M. and after he blew Debby's back out, Koran got a page from Lil' L: "Yo, Love, I'm going to have to cut this short. Do ya thing, baby, the phone is over there, stop by again on Friday, you got my number in ya pager, it's the number with 68/69 next to it. Koran, don't get me mixed up with some of those other bitches out there, I know you know I'm feeling you."

"Yo, I'm out," said Koran. "Get with you later, keep it warm, keep it tight."

Lil' L told Koran to meet him by 181 by the ball courts in an hour.

"Cool, gives me enough time to swing by my crib and see if the drama is over."

Koran got home, all was quiet and Koran could tell from the TV being on in his mom's room that whatever they were fighting about must be over.

"So what's up, man?" Koran said as he pulled out a blunt and took a hit.

"Yo, I want us to hit that store over by our school."

"Nigger, if we hit that store what about?"

"Yo, just hear me out, Koran, in the back room of that store they hold money from numbers they run."

"And how do you know this?" Koran asked Lil' L.

"My little sister Stacey told me she heard one of her friends' older brothers saying when they were coming to get the money."

"So when do you want to do this?"

"I was thinking about next Thursday or Friday," as Lil' L got in his car.

"Fuck it, let's make it happen, yo, let me hold that Eric B and Rakim tape."

"Here, you can keep this, bless the mic to the gods, shit."

It was now Friday morning and Shawn, Randy, and Koran were on the corner of Springfield HS waiting on Lil' L.

"Yo, where is this nigger?" Shawn said, looking at Koran.

"Nigger, he'll be here a few minutes later."

Lil' L pulled up with a cat named Cory, who they all knew from around the way.

"So why this nigger here?" said Shawn.

"Look, nigger, it's too many doors to cover, plus he got us the guns and shit."

"Yo, fuck the bullshit," said Koran, "if we're going to do this, then let's cut all this other shit! Randy, you stay with me and keep ya fucken' eyes open. Question, Cory, where did these guns come from?" asked Koran.

"Nigger, they're clean, motherfucker, they better be," said Koran, "and if by any chance the police end up at my house, nigger, I'll be waiting in ya living room when ya come home."

"So are we ready, nigger, let's do it," Shawn said.

"Count to ten, then we rush the store, get the fuck on the floor, get the fuck on the floor!" yelled Lil' L. "Yo, pass me the duct tape, watch these niggers."

Koran signaled Randy as he taped the hands and feet of the people in the store. Lil' L looked at Shawn and Cory as they make their way to the back of the store.

"Wait, nigger," Lil' L said as Cory ran to the back and kicked the door.

Bullets rang out, Cory took one to the arm.

"Fuck it, everybody in the back of the store! Batman, watch the front!" Lil' L said to Randy.

When Cory shot Shawn, Lil' L and Koran ran to the back.

"Let's get the money and get the fuck out of here. Yo, I think I hear the police coming," said Randy.

"Hit the back door and let's get the fuck out of here," said Koran. "We need to find a spot to go so we can count this money."

Lil' L looked at Koran and said, "Come on, I know where we can go."

About twenty minutes later, they pulled up by some chick named Angie who lived not too far away, her and Lil' L used to fuck off and on.

Shawn said to Lil' L, "Yo, I need to talk to you."

"What's up, man?"

"Yo, you brought this nigger Cory in, now we're hot, this nigger has to go."

Randy stepped in and said, "Yo, man, I ain't killen' nobody. Koran, what about you?"

Koran said, "Yo, he does have a point, but for right now let's count the money."

"So what's the total?"

"About $50,000," said Koran, looking at Lil' L.

"Okay, look, I need to break Shorty off for letting us come here. Cory, are you going to be okay? Oh, and Koran, we been hot and the streets been talking."

"Yeah, man, just help me up, I can go to my uncle's house, he won't be home until next week."

"Cool," said Shawn. "I'll drop you off, I'll get with you niggers later. Bye Koran, bye Shawn, bye Randy."

Angie looked at Lil' L, grabbed his dick, and said bye.

It was now around noon.

Koran said to Randy, "Yo, you still have those clothes in ya locker? Because we're going back to school like we don't know shit."

"You know they're going to kill Cory," Randy said as they left Angie's house and were now sneaking back in school.

"Come on, man, you know how this shit goes, hurry up, Randy."

As Koran got a girl he knew to open the back door.

"Yo, where are you going, Koran?" said Randy.

"Nigger, stop with all the fucken' noise, look, man, I use this locker for shit when I be hitten' niggers' pockets, put the money in there and go to class, yo, at 2 o'clock I'm going to come get you, if the police happen to come looking we have an alibi. Just chill, Randy, go to class like nothing never happened, don't forget to ditch those clothes from earlier. Look who I ran into, Randy, Mia and Charlene, and they trying to get high and fuck."

Randy looked at the both of them and smiled.

Koran leaned towards Randy and said, "We're going to the Jets Motel, nigger."

"For fucken'?" Randy replied.

"Look, we go there and chill the fuck out, didn't ya mom and them go somewhere so you don't have to go home? If that nigger Cory gets to talkin', you and me are nowhere to be found, now you understand?"

"Damn, you one smart motherfucker, Koran. Nigger, I'm just not ready to go to jail."

"A yo, I seen Sweet P again in the hallway, she told me to tell you hi."

"Get the fuck out of here," said Koran. "Nigger, you better get with her before one of those Boom Bash niggers do."

"We will talk about it later."

As Koran opened the cab door and smacked Mia on the ass. "Fuck them, nigger," Korans said.

"No, what you need to be doing is fucken' Sweet P sexy ass."

Beep, beep, beep.

"Shit!"

"What, nigger!"

"It's Lil' L."

"So see what he wants."

"Randy, go with them to the motel, I will catch you there, I'm about to see what L wants. Yo, what's up, L?"

"Yo, you see that shit on the news? Man, the police said it must have been drug related, when they went up in there they found a few pounds of weed and more money."

"Get the fuck out of here," said Koran. "Damn, if Cory didn't get all crazy on us we could have bagged all that shit."

"No bullshit, man, on another note we need to take care of Cory."

"Damn, that what you're hitting me about?"

"No, over the phone business, remember?"

"Chill, Koran, this line is clean. We can handle this later tonight. Shawn knows where he's at. A yo, I wanted to tell you but forgot, when we were up in that store I dropped some IDs of some nigger I robbed over by 243rd."

"Word," said Lil' L, "ya ass is always thinking, I'll page you later," Lil' L said and got off the phone.

"Jets Motel, how may I help you?"

"Room 305, please."

"Hello?"

"Hey, Randy, it's me, Koran, something came up."

"Is everything okay?" Randy asked.

"We good, man, you're about the closest thing I have to brother, shit, we go back since I first moved out to Queens and went to 181. Yo, man, you can stay at the motel with them as long as you want go home in the room is paid for."

"Where are you going, Koran?"

"I need to go see my sister. What's the number to Shack Cabs? It's okay, I got it."

Later on that night, Koran went to see his sister, who told her how her and her girls was at the Jamaican spot on Merrick and how Lil' L was running off with the mouth to some chick saying how he be running all y'all niggers.

"I just want you to know I think ya boy is a fucken' snake so watch ya back, I understand you think he's ya boy, but that nigger don't give a fuck about you."

"Good looking out, sis."

"Come on, K, you're my lil' brother, did you hear about that shit over by Springfield?"

"Na, what shit?" said Koran.

"The store got robbed, so where were you? Come on with that shit, you okay?"

"I'll get with cha later, sis."

"Watch your back, Koran, you know how niggers get down even more those that are jealous."

"I'm out, sis."

The bell rang. Kathy looked out the window and it was Koran.

"What's up, big head, be sure to check ya mailbox, page me if ya need me."

Kathy came downstairs and found some money in her mailbox, looked at her brother Koran, and said, "Thank you and be safe."

Koran jumped his gate and went into his house. Some new nigger was there, so he hit the kitchen and went to his room, laid on his bed looking at all his Bruce Lee posters, and said to himself, "I gots to get the fuck out of here." He reached under his mattress and got the mess tab he got from Jamaican Rob from around the corner and closed his eye to forget all the shit that happened today. Here it was about three in the morning, Koran got a page.

"Nigger, do you know what time it is?"

Lil' L said, "We be there in ten minutes."

A few minutes passed and Koran got up, threw some shit on, and went downstairs.

"So you ready for a 187?" said Shawn.

"We went by Randy house but it didn't look like anybody was home. So it's us three again, fuck," Lil' L laughed.

"If ya wondering the nigger has to go," said Shawn, "and if ya bitch ass ain't up to it, we got the nigger in the trunk, we brought him so you could finish him off."

Koran said, "You two niggers think this shit is TV? I'm in this shit for the money."

"Well, now ya in this shit for the long ride!" said Lil' L. "Little Criminals for life."

"Nigger, we rob shit, we ain't killers," said Koran to Lil' L and Shawn. "Any of you niggers ever kill somebody?"

"No, motherfucker," said Lil' L, "but tonight all three of us are about to earn our fucken' stripes!"

"This motherfucker is a problem, he can put a monkey wrench in our whole shit, and what about that bitch house we went to?" said Koran. "We're going to kill her too?"

"Motherfucker, ain't no turning back now, so whatever the fuck ya feelings suck it the fuck up; I never liked that nigger Cory anyway."

"So that's what this is about, you not liking a nigger? Plus you bring his ass to my house, what kind of shit is that?"

"Nigger, for your information I keep that trick Angie coked up, shit, that bitch can hardly remember her fucken' name."

"Well, her coked-up ass knew all our names earlier," said Koran.

"After we kill this nigger, these niggers out here will know we're not playin'," said Lil' L.

"Pull up in there," Shawn said, "this place is as good as any, plus it's foggy out here."

One by one they took turns shooting Cory. After it was done they dropped him in Brookfield Lake.

Lil' L said, "Nigger, at some point you were going to have to put down your lil' razor you always like using, and get dirty."

Well, nothing was more dirty than this, Koran thought. *Shit! I just killed a nigger! What a way to bring in turning seventeen. We all had did shit.* It was just killing Cory didn't feel right with Koran as if Lil' L wasn't telling him everything.

Only months later, Koran would find out the reason Lil' L and Shawn wanted Cory dead was because Cory had slept with Lil' L's younger sister and she told him he raped her when Lil' L found out, so Lil' L got Cory to come with them to do this job and even if he didn't get shot he would never live to see another day.

"Yo, let's go to IHOP," Shawn said. "I'm buying!"

"What will it be?" the waitress said.

Lil' L and Shawn ordered the ham and eggs and a cup of coffee.

"And you, sexy?" the waitress asked, looking at Koran.

"Yo, nigger, snap out of it!" said Shawn.

"I'll have the steak and eggs with a glass of grape juice, beautiful."

"You always calling a bitch beautiful, bullshit," said Lil' L. "Let me school you two niggers to something, no female wants to be called bitch, okay, that's why you niggers always paying for pussy, you don't know how to treat a female. This nigger has a few bitches calling him Beloved and he thinks he's a fucken' pimp. None of those bitches would fuck with you if yo ass wasn't getting money with me," laughed Lil' L.

"I'm out, niggers."

Koran left and went home. No one was there, not the first time, for he was used to his mother not being home by now. He jumped in the shower to wash the dirt off, took the clothes he wore, and burned then in the bathtub. He checked his stash box as he did every day and noticed all his money was gone and so was the nigger who his mother called her boyfriend.

Koran got dressed but first looked in his room to see what else was missing, he then popped another mess tab and called One-Arm Chris on the phone and told him he needed a gun and it needed to be clean and that he would be by to pick it up before 3 o'clock.

Koran thought about killing Cory and now he was thinking about killing his mother's boyfriend, yet this fucken' time it was personal.

"I needed that fucken' money so I could get out this madhouse, for shit here is crazy."

Without that money he would be stuck living there and stuck with some niggers he needed to get away from. Koran said, "Fuck school today," and called One-Arm Chris back to let him know he was going to come pick up the gun.

A few hours passed and at this point Koran had taken about two or three mess tabs and was drinking. Koran sat across the street from his house, waiting for his mother's so-called boyfriend, Lucky Chucky or whatever his name was, to come there, and when he did this would be the second time Koran would kill somebody. With tears in his eyes, Koran was telling himself, "This nigger has to fucken' go."

Hours passed and no boyfriend. Just when Koran was about to leave, Koran saw his mother's car pull up. Koran dipped behind some bushes, pulled back the hammer on the nine he got from One-Arm Chris, and waited to see who was in the car, but no boyfriend. After waiting another hour and still no boyfriend, Koran went in the house to use the bathroom and left the gun in his jacket on the bed.

After Koran came out he found his mother in his room, looking in his stuff and on the phone with his uncle, as she told him she just found weed in his room, hoping she did not pick up his jacket. She told Koran's uncle that the boy did what he wanted and that he thought he was grown, that all he did was eat and sleep all day, he needed to get a job.

Koran's mother handed him the phone and said, "Ya Uncle Steven wants to talk to you."

"About what?" Koran said.

"TAKE THE FUCKEN' PHONE!" yelled Koran's mother.

"Yo, hello!" said Koran.

"Yo, man, ya mother tells me she just found some weed in your room and that you haven't been going to school, do you need me to come out there and kick ya ass?" said his Uncle Steven.

After losing all his fucken' money, Koran was not thinking about his Uncle Steven or his mother's bullshit.

Koran said to his uncle, "She calls you to tell you about some weed in my room, did she call and tell you about the pound of weed that some nigger named Smalls dropped off here and left in her bedroom?"

Steven had nothing to say other than "Yo, man, you and ya mother need to try and get along," and got off the phone.

Koran grabbed his jacket and asked, "So where is ya boyfriend, Lucky Chucky or whatever his name is?"

His mother yelled back, "HE FUCKEN' LEFT!" then slammed the door.

"Damn, here it is, I just turned seventeen and I don't even get a happy birthday, I hate my fucken' life," Korans said.

After realizing he was now stuck there, he had no choice but to get in on the key or half a key Lil' L was talking about getting and pushing in Brookfield Park. Koran left and ran into his friend Tommy, who had been pushen' weed since Koran lived in Rosedale.

"So what's good, Koran?"

"Not a mother fucken' thing, man, I need to come the fuck up. Yo, Tommy, how much money do you make from selling dope of this ice cream truck?"

"What have I always told you, Koran? You never ask a man how much money he is maken', now you and ya L.C. Crew should be makin' a good penny from all the houses you're robbing. Oh, nigger, stop acting like I didn't know you were one of them, I watched ya come up, ya lil' young ass is still in school, which is good, you need a paper trail so the police and shit don't fuck with you. You can't just be out her like these niggers, that's how they get hot. Look, Koran, you like nice shit! I seen a lot of niggers come up living out here in Queens, some make it, some don't, look at me, I'm a nigger selling ice cream, right?"

"Yeah, I'm also the nigger all of Queens gets it dope from, with this ice cream truck I can go where I want, see and do what I want, fuck the police, I'm just a nigger selling ice cream. I tell you before you're my age, half the lil' niggers you think are your friends will either turn on you, trying to fuck ya girl or be mad because you maken' money and they standing there holding their dick."

"Now Koran, back to what I was saying, here you are in high school wearing a hundred-dollar Bally shoes, two and three beepers, sweatsuits and shit, drinking Moët, nigger, if ya wasn't doing something ya sure seem like it. Ya other two friends, Lil' L and Shawn, I seen them at a lil' spot I go to over by Rochdale projects, these fools are up in there like they run Queens, not knowing it was some real kills up in there, just laughing at them. You're smart, Koran, you just need to play ya cards right, if ya need something call me."

"Yo, Tommy, can you drop me off by 228th? I need to catch a cab."

"Hello, yo, what's up, Deb?"

"Hey, what's going on, Koran? You coming by?"

"Yeah, I was just seeing if you were home, I'm not one to just pop up on someone."

"Nigger, you mean you don't want to come by here and some other guy is here."

"Well, something like that," then got off the phone.

A few days later....

"Randy, what's going on, man?"

"Nothing, just been going to school and shit, my moms popped in on a few of my classes and told me if I miss another class she was going to tell my father."

"What's up with you, man?" said Randy.

Koran told Randy about his mother taking his money, then blacked out and then said, "Let's go get something to eat and nigger, if it's pork I'm not buying it!"

"Yo, ya ass is real funny, Koran, what did pork ever do to you? Yo, have you seen the paper?"

"Why, Randy?"

"I think that girl, what's her name was in there."

"What girl, nigger!" Koran asked Randy.

"Let's just get the paper and I'll show you. See, that's her, right?"

"That's her, nigger, it just says house caught on fire."

"Keep reading," Randy said.

"Oh, shit! It says girl dies in fire and the other one in hospital as a result of somebody smoking crack or some shit."

"Damn, kid, which one died?"

"It doesn't say, Randy."

"Damn, man, I was just with Deb, shit, a few days ago. Yo, what time is it?" asked Koran.

"It's almost 9 o'clock."

"Come on, man, we'll be late for school," Randy said.

"Nigger, McDonald's is right here and fucken' Spring Field right there, come on, man, you know what's her name will let us in."

"Damn, nigger, you hit that, Koran?"

"Na, man, she just likes me, I'll get with you at lunch."

Just then the police pulled up.

"Koran Biggs?"

"Yeah!"

"Get the fuck in the car, we want to question you about a shooting that took place last week."

"You can talk to me right here."

"Yo, Koran, you cool?" said Randy.

"Get ya punk ass out of here!" said one of the officers.

"It's cool, man, just try and find which one was in the fire," Koran said, then turned to the officers and said, "If you mother fuckers put ya hands on me I'll take ya ass to court."

"We just going to take you down to the 113th Precinct, motherfucker, so get ya ass in the damn car before we put some shit in ya pocket and charge you with drug possession!"

"So again, Koran, where were you last Friday at around 10 A.M., and motherfucker, don't say school because we checked."

"I keep telling you I don't know anything about somebody getting shot."

"Nigger, where the fuck were you?" said the officer. "I bet if I take ya ass in the back room you'll tell me."

"FUCK YOU! You think this is the first or last time I got my ass kicked by one of you pigs? If you got something on me then arrest my ass, if not I'm fucken' steppin'!"

"Koran, you think you're a real bad ass, don't you? You be lucky if ya ass even see 20."

Another officer walked in and said, "His prints don't match."

Koran smiled, looked at both officers, and said, "Get the fuck out my face."

"Koran, if I was you I'd watch your ass. I'll be watching ya friends too."

"And I'll be watching you watch us, pig. Yo, how am I to get back to school?"

"Drop his little ass back off a few blocks from here."

About 45 minutes later, "Mr. Koran Biggs, the principal would like to see you."

"Shit," Koran said, "this is not my fucken' day!"

Knock, knock.

"Come in, son. I'm going to get right to the point, ya fucken' up, now maybe you don't care about ya life, you need to start thinking about you future. I see a lot of kids come in and out of my office every day; now I don't know what you do out there on the street, I just know ya ass can't be as bad as some of the people in school have you out to be. I want you to remember this, son, you lay down with dogs, you'll get up with fleas. Close my door and take ya ass to class."

Funny white motherfucker always riding a nigger, Koran thought as he walked out the principal's office.

"Hi, 59."

"Hey, Sweet P, how are you doing?"

"I'm okay, so why you keep ducken' me?"

"Me, ducken' you?"

"Yeah!"

"You know I do have a name?"

"I know, your name is Koran. I also know you and your little friends are troublemakers, I only called you 59 so you would say something."

"Go to class, Koran, you too, Ms. Fuller," said the principal.

"Damn, so he knows you too? I see you're not as good as you would like people to think you are, do you think I can have your number?"

"I don't have a pen or a piece of paper."

"Give me your hand, Koran, you better call me!"

"Yo, I got to get to class; I'll meet you outside after school, peace, love."

2:30 and school was letting out.

"So 59, sorry, Koran, what took you so long?"

"Pardon me, I ran into somebody I know."

"Yeah, probably a girl."

"Damn, ya funny, and no, it wasn't a girl, so can I walk you home? I mean, we're going in the same direction."

"Yo Koran! Yo Koran! Hold on."

"What, nigger!"

"Oh, my bad, kid."

"Randy, chill out. Randy, this is Sweet P, this is my boy Randy. Yo, man, I'm like in the middle of something."

"About time, nigger; I'll get with you later."

"Sweet P, where do you live?"

"I live off of Farmers."

"Yeah, I know, with your grandmother," Koran said.

"Well, I live with my grandmother because my mother couldn't handle me, so I stay with my grandmother."

"I ain't mad at you, love, I been there before," Koran said.

"So what else you know about me?"

"I know I'm happy to be walking you home."

"I'll see you tomorrow, Koran, peace, love."

Beep, beep, beep.

"Yo, what's up, man?"

"Nothing, man, yo, did you and Shawn do anything last week?"

"Anything like what?"

"Look, Lil' L, the fucken' police picked me up today, asking me something about a shooting."

"Na, nigger, I don't know shit."

"What about Shawn?"

"I haven't seen Shawn since that thing we did."

"So what the police say?" Lil' L asked.

"They just kept asking me where was I and something about a jacket, then another cop came in and was like my prints don't match. Yo, L," said Koran, "I was asking you about the shit because I know you always like to wear those bright-ass Adidas jackets and thought maybe it was you they were looking for and because I know it's not me they wanted."

"Hold the fuck up!" Lil' L said. "You let him hold your jacket the other night so you can kill that bullshit."

"Oh, shit, that nigger does have my jacket, I need to go up on 228th and see if this nigger is up there."

"What the fuck! Look at all these fuckin' police cars. A Divine, what the fuck happen?"

"A yo, the police just killed ya boy Shawn, get the fuck out of here, Divine. Nigger, that's his mother over there crying, nigger tried to rob the wrong niggers and they blasted his ass; the police caught his brother, they say he shot one of them and tried to run."

"Yo, Lil' L, that's the fucken' cop who was talken' to me earlier, yo man, I'm out of here. Peace!"

The next morning Randy went to Koran's house and called him out the window. "Yo, Koran, Koran, come downstairs."

"What's wrong, man?"

"Ask Koran, yo, I founded out about the shit with the fire. Well, it turns out it was Mia in the fire and Debby was the one who got burnt. Some nigger at school was saying that some cat was giving her weed laced with crack, so it wasn't long before that shit started calling her. I'm going to need for you and my sister to go see her, I'll pray for her."

"Yeah, you do, man, you do that, Randy. So what's with all those people at your house, Randy?"

"They want to buy our house."

"No bullshit," Koran said.

"Yeah, man, if they buy our house they will knock all of that shit down over there and build some new shit."

"Damn, man, so where are you moven' to, or are you staying in Queens?" Koran asked.

"I gots to go wherever they go, Koran, I hope you not mad but I gave most of the money to my church."

"Look, man, you gave your money to a God up there when it's people down here who are starving every day. I'm not mad at you, man, to each his own," said Koran. "I just know with all the shit going wrong in my life, given' my money to some church that has more money than I do is not something I would have done, shit! As if God was ever broke."

"Nigger, you going to hell," said Randy.

"My brother, I'm liven' there now, ya just don't know," Koran said, then told Randy, "Let's go play some ball, so I can whip ya ass."

"Go get ya ball, nigger, and I see you around the corner."

"Oh, it's on then," and Koran ran upstairs to get his ball.

Two months later Randy moved and now it was just Koran and Lil' L. Lil' L dropped out of school, striving to be the next Neno Brown, and got picked up for some bullshit and got hit with a year, trying to live off of his brother's rep.

"Koran, so when are we going out, all you want to do is hang with ya boys? You're not fucken' ya boys! I don't even like Lil' L ass; I keep telling you his ass is trouble," said Sweet P. "You and me have been going out for almost two years, and my grandmother wants to know how come she hasn't meet you yet?"

"Yo, come on with that shit, those niggers are like family," said Koran. "As to us going out, you know how shit is with my family and I'm only doing this shit. Look, my family may seem all nice and shit to you, but you don't know shit what it was like growing up not knowing where your mother was, family given' you drugs and shit. Baby, go to class before you're late and we'll do something soon, okay?" said Koran.

"We better!" yelled Sweet P.

School was out and Sweet P was standing outside waiting for Koran.

"Koran, I don't care what you're about to do, but you taking me home so if this cab ain't for us it is now."

That cab stopped right off of Farmers Blvd., just on the corner of that pizza spot where Koran, Lil' L, and Shawn set it off on some niggers about four years go for trying to take Shawn's chain.

"Damn, it feels funny as hell to be over here," said Koran. "What did you ask, Sweet P?"

"Oh, nothing."

So they got to Sweet P's grandmother's house, and not only was her grandmother there, her mother stopped by and said, "So this is the famous Koran."

"Koran, my grandmother wants to know if you're staying for dinner."

"What did she make, because I don't eat pork?"

"What's wrong with pork?" said Sweet P's mother. "What are you, a Muslim?"

"No, I'm—"

"He just doesn't eat pork!" said Sweet P. "Koran, my grandmother made pork shops," said Sweet P.

"Shit, I'm not eating that, you just be sure to brush real good after you eat that swine before touching my lips. Sorry, Mrs. Fuller, but I have to go, nice meeting you."

"You be sure to stop by again, for I haven't had a real chance to talk to you."

"Sweet P, walk me to the door. Damn, ya mom seems like she's on some real keeping you on lockdown shit," said Koran. "What's up with all the damn questions? I'm going to walk up the street and get something to eat and go to the crib, I'll call you later. Yo, let me get an order of five chicken wings and some shrimp fried rice."

"A yo, your name is Koran?"

"Who are you?"

"Peace, my name is Dolla, if you don't mind after you get you food could I speak to you for a minute?"

"So, what's up, man?"

"Na, nothing much, yo, I was wondering if you could put a brother on?"

"Put a brother on with what?" said Koran.

"I'm going to be real, these niggers around here, shit is garbage."

"Walk with me to the liquor store," said Koran. "Yo, let me get two bottles of Moët; shit, I forgot my damn orange juice."

"Moët, orange juice, and Chinese food, what?"

"Baby, you know another way to eat this?" said Koran. "I told Sweet P I wanted to talk to you before when you came around here. What's your name again?"

"Dolla."

"And you live where?" asked Koran.

"I live over on 110 and Farmers." Dolla told Koran, "Yo, give me ya math and I'll get back to you."

"I'm going to have to cut this short, my ride is here," Koran said and pulled off in his favorite cab.

"So what's good, baby?" said the cab driver.

"Nothing much, just trying to make it out here, ya know," said Koran, "just came from my girl crib, the whole fucken' Klan was there, and to top it off they were about to eat pork, shit, I had to get up out of there," laughed Koran.

A week later Koran ran into Lil' L's sister Stacey, and she told him, "You know my brother will be coming home soon."

"Yeah, I was around the way and somebody told me that."

"Koran, how come you never tried talken' to me? I mean, even after I tried given' you the ass?"

"The difference between me and your brother is there are lines I just don't cross, you need something I got you, as for as the sex goes I'm good, plus you're just a kid to me; ya want another reason? My name is not Cory. You got that nigger killed over some bullshit and ya punk-ass brother had to get me to do it."

"Yo, Koran, I'm sorry," said Stacey. "I just wanted my brother to fuck him up, I didn't know y'all were going to kill him."

"Cut the shit, Stacey! When have you known ya brother to play when it comes to you? Think about that. You hear from your brother, tell him to call me, I have to go," said Koran.

It was Friday and Koran felt like seeing his grandmother, it'd been some time since he seen her, so he gave her a call and told her he'd be there soon.

"Damn, everything has changed," Koran said to himself as he rode in the cab to Brooklyn to go see his grandmother. "Shit is crazy out here, Shawn is dead, and Randy has moved, Lil' L is in jail; right now the best thing in my life is Sweet P, but shit, how long will that last? A female like that and a nigger like me, I see me going in one direction and her in a direction I'm not ready to go."

"Yo, Koran, we're here!" said the cab driver.

"I'm a call you in about an hour, maybe two, keep the change, nigger, yo know how we do," said Koran.

"Can you press the 12th floor, please?" as Koran stepped in the elevator.

The doorbell rang.

"Who is it?"

"It's your grandson!"

"Who?"

"Your grandson, Koran!"

His grandmother, Peaches, opened the door and said to him, "Do you want anything to eat?"

"No," answered Koran.

"Yeah ya ass probably eat all that fast-food shit before coming here," said his grandmother.

"I'm okay, I'm just not hungry," said Koran.

"So have you been staying out of trouble?" asked his grandmother. "I don't have a number to call you, and when I talk to ya mother she acts like I don't know how to use the phone."

"I've been okay, I be right back, I'm going to the bathroom."

"Don't bring none of that shit in my house and have the police come up in here and take my lil' bite of money I got!" said his grandmother, Peaches.

"I'm just going to the bathroom."

"So what, you come here to get the rest of you stuff?" his grandmother asked.

"No, I just thought I'd come see you."

"You spoke to your mother?"

"No, not since her ass hit me with that stick and almost broke my arm," said Koran.

"Since you don't come pick me up from the subway anymore, I started coming home from work with another lady in my building. You know that boy that you used to play with got shot in the foot last week?" said his grandmother.

"How would I know that? I don't live here."

"I haven't spoken to ya mother since she almost broke ya arm, she knows she was wrong for haven' some nigger in my house, then she's going to take it out on you because you tell me," said his grandmother..

"I try not to think about that stuff," said Koran.

Beep, beep, beep.

"What's that?" said his grandmother.

"It's my pager!" Koran told her.

"Her ass called here the other day, talking about 'Oh, Peaches, if you speak to so-and-so can you tell them to call me,' like her ass think I don't have anything else to do," said his grandmother. When are you going to church with me?" she asked Koran.

"I don't know," Koran said, "can I use your phone?"

"Is it long distance, for you know I don't need my phone bill being high," his grandmother said.

"No, it's not a long-distance call, I'm only calling somebody up the street," Koran said. "Yo, Blue, what's the deal, baby? Okay, I'll hit you back in a minute," and then Koran got off the phone.

"I don't know why every time y'all come here first thing y'all do is get on my damn phone," said his grandmother as she went in the kitchen. "You sure you don't want to eat? It's not pork," she said as she sat down to have a drink.

"Oh, I have something for you," said Koran.

"Is it money, because you know I don't have anybody helping me pay all these bills," she said.

"No, it's a bottle of E & J, you still drink that?" said Koran.

"Yeah, I had a bottle over there, then ya Uncle Steven came by and drank my damn bottle and then says, 'I'll buy you another one.'"

"Well, I have to go, Peaches," said Koran as he stood by the door.

"Stop by sometime, I sure could use your help cleaning this house," as she gave her grandson a kiss and a hug.

As Koran left his grandmother and thought back to when he used to live there and remembered the time some lil' nigger took his Pumas outside his grandmother's building; shit was funny for a week, later that same person was found dead with a gunshot to the back of the head in another building.

Koran realized so much had changed and got on the elevators.

"So what's your name?"

"Pardon me?"

"Yeah, I'm talking to you, Mr. Smell Good," she said.

"How old are you?" Koran asked.

"Old enough," the girl said.

"Well, ya too damn young for me," and stepped off the elevator.

"Shit! I forgot to call Blue back," Koran said as he walked across the street to use the payphone.

"Yo, peace!"

"Blue, be in front of your house in about 15 minutes."

Koran stepped out of the cab and shook Blue's hand.

"Damn, nigger, you a hard man to keep in touch with," said Blue.

"Yo, man, I just been on the grind; so how's the cipher doing?" Koran asked.

"All is peace on this end, so when are you going to take some of that money and buy something to drive?" asked Blue.

"Not sure, having a car is just another way for niggers to know when I'm coming or where I'm at," said Koran.

"Yo, if you ain't doin' shit or got somebody upstairs, let's go shopping, for I could use a few more pair of Ballys."

"So what, we're going to catch the train, if so it's right up the street," said Blue.

"Fuck a train, man! We can jump in a cab and be downtown faster," said Koran.

"I see you're still a pretty motherfucker," said Blue.

"Not at all, I just like riding with my feet up and shit," said Koran.

"Yo, it's always good to see fam," said Blue, "and thanks for the watch."

Beep, beep, beep.

"Yo, Blue, I have to go, man, it's my girl. My cab should be here soon, I'll call you later, that's my word, peace!"

"So where to, Koran?" the cab driver said.

"Back to Queens, first stop at the liquor store up the block, need to get another bottle of Moët."

Twenty minutes passed and Koran pulled up at his girl's house and saw Dolla.

"Peace, baby, what's good?"

"Waiting on you, Dolla."

"Yo, you and me are going to do something real soon, just let me take care of something else I'm working on first."

Koran went to his girl's house and saw her older sister.

"What's up, big head?"

"Damn, Koran, how many pair of Ballys do you have?"

"I could never have enough, love, where's ya sister?" said Koran.

"I'm right here, baby, here you go with ya Moët and crazy straw," Sweet P said. "My mom is haven' a cookout today and I want you to come."

"It's cool, I'll be there," said Koran. "Yo, get ya shit and let's go to the telly," Koran said to Sweet P.

"I can't, I have to help my mother, but after the cookout I can go."

"Okay, that's cool, look, I'm about to slide, I'll call you when I'm on my way, peace, love."

My mother always said I'd be like my father, her ass was so fucking wrong, I'm not even half her age and make more money than she do, Koran thought as he was on his way back to his own apartment over in Rosedale.

Years had passed, but the game was still the same. Koran was now 18. Rule number one within the game, get that money even if it kills you, and after Koran came up the way he did as a child him being broke was out of the question. To stay on point, Koran would hit a pocket here and there, then give it back just to stay on point, or he would read books on alarms so he always knew when the new alarms came out.

It was 3:30 and Sweet P called.

"Baby, I'll be there in a minute, I just need to throw something on and pick something up for the cookout."

About an hour later, Korans showed up with bottles of Moët and some other stuff for the cookout and said to Sweet P, "There's a box of Moët in the cab."

A couple of drinks and a few hours later, Sweet P asked Koran, "What's wrong?"

"You have a real cool family here, this is some shit I don't know anything about, when it comes to mine all mother fuckers do is talk about each other, then act like shit is all good when they see that person." Koran paused for a minute and fell out.

He woke up the next day in Sweet P's bed and her older sister standing over him, saying, "Good morning, my sister left some food for you in the kitchen."

"Damn, my head is ringing," said Koran, "how much did I drink last night?"

"You don't remember me and my sister bringing you upstairs?"

"What little I do remember about last night, I don't think ya sister would want me telling you. What time is it, big head?"

"It's almost 9:30."

"Where is your sister, big head?"

"She went to get the newspaper; yo, I need for you to call this number and ask for #7, tell them my name and give them your address."

"Tell ya sister I left some money upstairs and to call me when she gets back."

"A Tommy, what's going on, man?"

"Nothing much, Koran, same old shit, just a different day. Ain't ya ass up kind of early?" said Tommy.

"I was on my way home, I was just going to run in the store real quick to get some juice and a newspaper."

"I heard that, so when are you going to ask that fine-ass girl of yours to live with you?"

"Come on, Tommy, you always taught me to keep maken' money and my private shit not together. You of all people know I've done a lot of shit out here with and without those niggers I call family, don't need any nigger out here trying to get back at me by fucken' with her; that's why I live in one place and here in another and none of the people I fuck with know where she lives. Tommy, I'm about to break out, man."

"A Koran, you be careful out here; take some of that money and buy some property, don't be like these niggers out here gots cars and shit but still liven' with their mamas."

"Damn, Tommy has always been looking out for me," said Koran, "for as long as I have been living out here in Queens, shit is crazy, he has been more of a father to me than my own father; shit, I don't remember shit about my father but his name, I just know when I have kids I plan to do more for them than his bitch ass has ever done for me. Shit is weird, how I seem to find more love in the street with niggers than with people who are supposed to be family."

Just then a car pulled up and two niggers jumped out, one Koran seemed to remember from somewhere but couldn't remember where.

One said, "You don't remember me?" and shot Koran and said, "Life's a bitch," and jumped in the car.

As Koran fell to the ground he managed to get off a few shots, shooting one in the neck.

"Koran! Koran!" yelled Tommy. "What the fuck happen, man? Shit, how bad is it?"

"Get me up," said Koran, "before the police come, help me up, Tommy! Yo, Tommy, get me the fuck out of here, man, lil' bitch-ass nigger couldn't even step to me, he shot at me when my back was turned! From across the fucken' street," said Koran.

"Did you see who it was?" said Tommy.

"Yeah, I know who they are, just get me out of here, lucky I had my vest on you gave me."

"Shit, nigger, I never take mine off," said Tommy. "So who the fuck was it?"

"The nigger that shot me, I don't know, but the nigger who was with him was a nigger I had took his bullshit ring, didn't think that nigger would come back like that over a ring," said Koran. "I only got a couple of hundred for it," he told Tommy. "Yo, this is not the way to my house, where the fuck we're going?"

"Ya ass is like a son to me, taken' you to my doctor to make sure you're okay," Tommy said, "don't know how many times I have to tell you when you start something make sure you finish shit."

"But Tommy, that shit was a couple of months ago," said Koran.

"Now you see why I say you never go home the same way and ya always stay on point out here, just lay there, we're almost there," said Tommy.

An hour passed.

"So Doc? What's the story?"

"Tommy, he needs to stay in bed. I wrapped up his ribs and gave him something for the pain, it's a damn good thing he had that vest on."

"Yo, Koran, I want you to go to this address, it's one of my spots, and stay there for a few days, I'll call you like tomorrow and we can figure out what to do about these niggers that shot you."

It was 4 A.M. and the phone rang at the house where Koran was.

"Hello?"

"Yo, this is Tommy, just wanted you to know those niggers who shot you are taken' a dirt nap, found them niggers over by Springfield, stay there as long as you like, just make sure you leave the key under the doormat."

"A Tommy, man—"

"Don't even go there," Tommy said and hung up the phone.

Two days later Koran went back home and saw he had a few messages on his machine and noticed he had a message from Dolla, telling him he heard from his girl that he was shot and that he was just calling to see if a brother was okay.

Koran picked up the phone and called Sweet P. "Hey, baby, what's goin' on?"

"Where are you, Koran? You get shot and nobody hears from you. Koran, did you tell Dolla to stop by and check on me, because since you got shot he was coming by my house like two, three times a day, asking me and my sister do we need anything and asking about you."

"He's good people, baby, don't stress it," said Koran. "So you said he came by and was making sure everything was okay and how I was? I'm okay, baby, I had my vest on, my ribs just hurt a little but I'm good. Love, need for you to tell him I said good looken' out and I will not forget it, I'll swing by your house around six, I just need to lay down first."

Koran called cab #7. "Yo, man, I need for you to be over here in a few, need to go to my girl's crib. A yo, nigger, when you stop by bring me something to eat."

"Like what?" said the cabdriver.

"I don't know, some curry goat something, man; remember, don't be late, need to be there by six."

It was about 5:15 and the cab pulled up.

Ring, ring.

"Hello?"

"Yo, Koran, I'm outside," said the cabdriver.

"On my way, man," and he grabbed his keys and another clip for his nine, then jumped in the cab. "Yo, this fucken' food is slamming, man, good looken' out, that shit hit the spot, yo, pull up right there, I'll get out right here. Yo, Dolla, come here, man!"

"Oh, shit, man, what's up, Koran?"

"Yo, man, I thought about what we spoke on, plus I also know how you been kind of looken' out for Short and her family. I'm going to set you up over here, now you know these little niggers like Dee and them will start acting funny as soon as they see, you ain't fucken' with them anymore, just want you to do this for me. Don't do shit where ya live and you continue to look out for me and mine and I'll do the same from here on out, we're family; now I doubt if you run into any beef over here but if you do call me," said Koran, then walked to the corner store for a bag of Bontons and something to drink.

"Koran, you know you had me worried," said Sweet P. "When I heard what happened I didn't know what to do, Koran, you need to grow up, for I can't keep doing this shit, you got niggers around here acting like it's all about you and your friends."

"Yo, look, the only friends I have is this mother fucken' nine and you."

"I want more than what I have, is that a problem?"

"Look, I don't need this shit, okay?" said Koran.

"What happened to the person I met a couple of years ago? You're changing, Koran, and I don't like it, I'm going in the house."

"You act like I'm out here doing this shit just to be doing it, as if I want to be doing this shit forever, talk to you later," said Koran.

It'd been about a week or more since Koran and Sweet P saw each other, and no matter what happened between them in the back of Koran's head he felt she was right, feeling like he couldn't eat and Koran dropped out of school and made a crime a fulltime job. Plus he knew it wasn't going to be long before he was kicked out another school.

It was 1 A.M. and Koran's pager was blowing up.

"Who the fuck is this?" said Koran.

It was Dolla paging him to tell him some nigger over there is talken' shit and had put his people on a block that belonged to Dolla.

"Yo, don't worry about nothing, let me make a phone call and tell him if and when you see a black Jetta hit the block, leave because shit is about to get hot."

A half an hour later Koran called Dolla and said, "Your lil' problem is taken care of," and hung up the phone. That was the last time Dolla or Koran had a problem with anybody else over there. Just as he hung up the phone, Koran got a call from Lil' L saying to come to Brookfield Park at 3 o'clock tomorrow.

"Yo, man, don't you know what time it is? Shit, ain't you still upstate?" said Koran.

"Nigger, I been home about a week now."

"Man, call me tomorrow," Koran said and hung up.

Not being able to go back to sleep, Koran started to think about the fight him and Sweet P had, him getting shot, him feeling like he didn't have a father nor knew his mother, and how it seemed just like yesterday he was on his way to class, now he was breaking into people's homes and bagging shit in plastic bags.

"Damn, the only fucken' time I seem happy is when I'm high or with Sweet P, yet nothing last forever," he said to himself as he sparked up a blunt he just rolled.

It was 3 o'clock and he didn't see Lil' L.

"Damn, I hate when niggers say one thing and do something else."

Just as Koran was about to leave, Lil' L showed up.

"What's up, Koran?"

"Sank or swim," said Koran.

"You know how it is. I've been watchin' niggers in this park and I think we should set up shop in here."

"Damn, you ain't been home a month and the first thing that comes out ya fucken' mouth is setting up shop," he said.

"Can you think of something better, nigger?" said Lil' L. "What, you want me to go get a job at McDonald's or some fucken' carwash, Koran? This is what a nigger knows, remember, it was me who put you the fuck on, Koran, not the other way around," said Lil' L. "What, some bitch made you soft? Oh, then again you never did have a lot of heart."

"A yo, L, don't get it twisted, we both made each of money, your problem is you think niggers is supposed to follow yo ass around like a helpless dog or some shit."

"I ain't never been a yes nigger."

"So you think just because you went to jail that makes you a big fucken' man, L? I was smart enough not to get caught and go to jail, that's you, Mr. Flashy and shit, always wanting to be seen, and if you must know ain't no pussy got me to where I can't think for myself," said Koran. "Look around you, shit has changed, nigger, we ain't little no fucken' more, L. Like I said, what's it going to be, man, Lil' L?" asked Koran. "I'm in, man, nigger," and he walked away.

"Trust me, Koran, you won't be sorry," Lil' L said and walked in the other direction.

Over the next couple of months, Lil' L and Koran took out one crew after another and every other week him and Sweet P were breaking up. She told Koran, "At some point you have to stop this shit and grow up," that it would not be long before he ended up in jail or dead.

Koran, feeling like he was stuck between the girl he loved and loyalty to Lil' L, he found himself not knowing what do to and started drinking more and sniffing coke.

"Yo, Koran, you remember that time we all cut school and we pissed in that 40-oz bottle and that nigger that wanted to be down so bad was like 'I'll drink it'?"

"Yeah, nigger, I remember y'all niggers doing that shit, I remember him licking I think the bottom of your sneakers on the bus," said Koran.

"Whatever happened to him?" said Lil' L.

"Not sure, man, I think the last time I saw him he was going to the principal's office for being drunk and shit."

"Damn, I remember I wanted to fuck Mrs. Young," said Lil' L.

"Damn, she was fine as hell too," said Koran and started laughing. "I remember all of us being at a hotel one night and you leaving me there with some crackhead-looking strippers thinking that shit was funny, talking about they were for me and you were coming right back," said Koran.

"Damn, nigger, you don't forget shit, do you? You still on that no-pork shit because a nigger is hungry, Koran? We can go eat, let's go to that Jamaican spot," Lil' L said. "Yo, man, what you know about the dope game?"

"I know I'm not fucken' with it," Koran said. "I know I'm doing okay with what I got; we come a long ways from the two of us liven' together and worked for that crackhead Dread."

"I want more," said Lil' L. "Shit, I want more."

"What the fuck is it you want?"

"I want the world, nigger, and everything in it."

"Bullshit, nigger, I'm not going to be doing this shit forever."

Beep, beep, beep.

"Yo, L, I'll be right back."

"Who the fuck is that? Some bitch got ya noise all open?" said L.

"Nigger, have you even gotten some pussy since you been home, or all you know how to use is ya hand?" Koran then got up and dialed the number on his car phone. "Yo, what's up, love?"

"Koran, I want to see you," said Sweet P.

"I'll come by there in about an hour."

"Okay, I'll see you then."

"Pardon me, waitress, could I have another Corona and the check?" Koran said.

Beep, beep, beep.

Damn, nigger, yo, shit just keeps blowen' up," said Lil' L.

"I'm just trying to be like you, L," said Koran and went to make his phone call.

"Yo, Koran, it's Tommy, come by my place, I need to talk to you about something."

"Okay, Tommy, I'm on my way."

Lil' L and Koran were leaving the restaurant when bullets started flying and they found themselves in the middle of a shootout.

"Yo, yo, L, you okay, man!!!"

Koran pulled out an M11 and shot back. "Yeah, nigger, these niggers bring a fucken' knife to a gun fight," and stood away from the car and yelled, "DEATH BEFORE DISHONOR!"

"Who the fucks are you, John Wayne? Nigger, look at you," said Lil' L. "I see ya ass put down that razor you always carried and got some big-boy shit. I see after getting shot that shit will change a person. Let's get the fuck out of here before the cops come."

Him and Koran jumped in the car.

"Yo, drop me off back at my car, if that's cool?" Koran needed to go see what Tommy wanted and always remembered to always come alone.

Lil' L pulled off, wondering where the hell was Koran going as he looked in the rearview mirror as he saw Koran one minute and gone the next.

The bell rang and it was Koran at Tommy's house.

"Come in," said Tommy, "the door is open."

Koran walked in and found Tommy at his bar having a drink.

"Yo, Koran, sit down, I'll get right to the point, you want a drink?" asked Tommy.

"Yeah, man, I'm drinking whatever you're haven'," said Koran.

Tommy handed Koran his drink and noticed he had glass in his hair and asked, "What the hell you been up to?"

"Why do you say that, Tommy?"

"Because you have some glass in ya hair."

"Oh, just before I came here me and L got into a shootout with some niggers over by that Jamaican spot."

"Wait, you brought that nigger Lil' L to my house?" said Tommy.

"Come on, man, you know I would never do no shit like that, he dropped me off at my car, we good."

Tommy and Koran never shared what they talked about to anyone, they were both funny like that.

"Just checken'," said Tommy, "now back to this shootout."

"When we were walking out, some niggers just started shooting, I don't know who they were," said Koran.

"Like man, this is what I wanted to talk to you about, ya boy Lil' L has been asking a lot of people about where to get some dope from, now for as long as I've known you and been watching him that nigger is as crooked as a fucken' snake. Plus I'm saying to myself, why does this nigger want to know about dope when Little Criminals are into B.N.E.s and the crack game?" said Tommy.

"Look, Tommy, I never lied to you, whatever he's doing it has nothing to do with me," said Koran.

"I know that my people told me this is some shit that ya partner is doing on his own. Koran, I want you to know something, if that nigger crosses the line and keeps sticking his noise where it shouldn't be, I will have no choice but to kill him," said Tommy.

"I have to go," said Koran, "I need to go see my girl." Koran knew in this game shit was never personal.

After hearing all of that and plus getting into a shootout, Koran found the first liquor store and got a bottle of Hennessy, jumped out his car, then called a cab.

It was now two hours later and he was just getting to Sweet P's house.

"I didn't think you were coming," she said as she stood there looking at Koran getting drunk. "You're not going in my house like that," she said.

"So what the hell did you want me to come here for if you're not going to let me in?" Koran said.

"I wanted to see you but not fucken' drunk, and why the fuck are you have a gun?"

"Look, I'm dealing with a lot of shit!"

"Okay, Koran!"

He took another drink. "You have no idea what it's like to be me."

Just then Dolla came walking down the street. "Hey, what's up?" said Dolla.

"You need to take his ass home," then she closed her door to her house.

Dolla got Koran a cab and said, "You need to go home."

"Wait, I want to talk to you," said Koran. "Look, man, don't ever be like me, and be sure to look out for her," then he told the driver to pull off. Koran was now living in Flushing Queens; he thought it was best to move after that shit with him getting shot before.

"Damn, it's good to be home," Koran said as he was greeted by his Boxer, Prince, then cut the TV on. Not too sure what to make of any of the things that happened tonight, Koran went to bed and told himself he would figure all this shit out in the morning.

It was 8:30 A.M. and Koran got woken up by his dog and he saw on TV they were talking about the shooting where him and L were at.

Still half awake, he started to remember the conversation between him and Tommy and started to think about how Lil' L brought up the conversation with him about selling dope. So Koran called Lil' L and asked him to meet with him at 181 Park around noon.

"So why did you want to meet over here, man?" said Lil' L.

"Not sure, I haven't been around here since I moved and my sister moved to South Carolina. Yo, so who do you think those niggers were from the other night?" Koran asked Lil' L.

"Who knows, man, it could be a number of people, Phat Boy and them or even some nigger from up the street on 228th trying to make a name. Yo, I may have a dope connect," said L. "I'm just going over a few things right now."

"Yo, how did you know I got shot?" Koran asked Lil' L.

"I don't know, man, somebody told me, I think my sister. After the shit with us the other night, I was thinking about having Sha be out there in the park and you just get the money from him."

"I'll think about it," said Koran. "Yo, how about us seating up a cab service where niggers call in there, get high, and we have drivers who bring them only what they wanted just like a real cab?" said Koran.

"And where do we get the cars?" Lil' L said to Koran.

"That shit ain't no problem, we get them from out of state for next to nothing, this way we keep our people out the ran off the block and we don't make shit no hotter than what it seems like it is now, for I don't need the Feds in my shit."

"Things seem to be running smooth with the changes," Koran said to Lil' L.

The buzz on the street was Koran and Lil' L must be on some other shit, for cats couldn't figure out just how they were maken' all that money and not haven the police fuck with them.

"Yo, L," said Koran, "I want you to know this if that nigger Sha turns out to be a snake, his ass has to go."

A month or so passed and Koran was still thinking about how in the hell did Lil' L know he was shot, and also why would L punch him in the same place? With Koran and Sweet P's relationship falling apart, Koran called her and asked her to come to Brookfield Park.

Koran told here to come there, for he needed to see someone and it would only take a second. He then paged Sha and told him to have his ass in the park and to be on time, and if something went wrong he was going to kill him. Koran saw Sweet P by the swings and asked her to please wait right here. Koran and Sha spoke for a minute and Sha then handed Koran some money. Koran headed to where Sweet P was and got stopped by a cop.

"You're under arrest," an officer said to Koran, then called for more backup.

"Yo, Sweet P, go home," said Koran, "don't worry about shit."

Back at the 113th Precent....

"Oh, if it isn't Mr. Koran Biggs, you know you fucked up this time, we got ya boy in the next room telling everything, your ass is about to take a trip to the booty house."

"You got me on what, nigger, I'm clean!" said Koran.

"Nigger, ya think so, well, ya boy Sha seems to have another store to tell and with the amount of shit he had, oh, yeah, you're going to jail, so don't drop the soap."

"I need to make my one phone call. Yo, Tommy, this is K, yo, man, the ice cream has melted. I'm at the 113th on some bullshit, I haven't seen a judge so I'm not sure how much my bail is just yet."

"I got you, I'll have my lawyer come down there now; you didn't have anything on you, did you?"

"Na, man, but that say they got somebody down here who can finger me."

"Don't say shit, my lawyer's name is Peter Wolf."

"Tommy, good looken' out, man," said Koran.

"Don't mention it. I told you my lawyer was good, so what happened?"

"I went to go pick up some money and some nigger gets bagged and I get pinched leaving the park. All I had was a few hundred on me," Koran said to Tommy.

"That shit don't seem strange to you, and where was ya boy Lil' L at?"

"He wasn't there."

"Wasn't there? So if he wasn't there, why the hell were you, Koran?" said Tommy. "Sounds to me like that nigger played you or is playing you. So when do you go back to court?"

"I go back October the 17th," said Koran.

"Koran, watch ya boy, I keep telling you that something smells fishy as hell."

"Yo, Tommy, you know the night I told you me and Lil' L got in that shootout, that nigger did something real strange like, he hit me right where I got shot at and seeming like he was playing until he mention something about me being shot, but I never told him the crazy part of that shit is he said his sister told him I haven't seen her shit not since she told me he was getting out. He goes by Money but to me he will always be Lil' L."

"So what, you think he had something to do with you getting shot?" asked Tommy.

"Not sure, all this shit just seems strange to me," said Koran. "Yo, Tommy, I'm thinking about getting out, man, and just starting over somewhere out of New York and just raise a family, I'll talk to you later."

The next morning around 10 A.M., Koran got a call from Dolla asking if they could meet up on Jamaica Ave. by the donut spot because he needed to talk to him.

"Yo, man, is everything okay?"

"Yeah, man, I just need to talk to you."

"It's cool, I need to pick up some dog food anyway; give me about an hour and I'll be there," said Koran.

Koran hung up the phone and jumped in the shower, got dressed, grabbed something to eat, then called his cab driver #7.

"A yo, I need for you to stop at the pet store on the Ave. after you drop me off and then drop it off at my house for me, yo, you can keep the change."

The driver said, "Damn, Koran, this is 100 dollars."

"It's cool, man, just remember to pick up the right kind of dog food, you know where to leave it at, you can let me out here," said Koran and jumped out. "Yo, Dolla, over here. What's good, man?"

As Koran and Dolla shook hands, "Just trying to get this paper," said Dolla.

"Walk with me," said Koran.

"Yo, man, I asked you to hook up with me because I got a letter in the mail telling me I have to report for Army training soon," said Dolla.

"So let me get the straight," said Koran, "you're going in the Army and what, you want me to look after ya family? Am I right?"

"You're not mad?" said Dolla.

"Come on, how could I be mad for a nigger looking to better himself, just bring ya ass home in one piece and don't shoot ya self in the fucken' foot. You have to remember something, Dolla, over the years you have been like a brother to a nigger more so than the very niggers who I ran and run with, all I did was look out for you, yet I never asked for you to do anything that you were not doing for me," said Koran.

"I leave in about two weeks," said Dolla.

"Shit! If my life wasn't so fucked up I'd go with you," said Koran. "Enough about that shit, let's go eat, I'm buyen'," said Koran.

"So what's up with you and Sweet P?" said Dolla.

"Same old shit, she wants me there, yet it's like the fucken' streets be calling me and shit, and plus the life I'm liven' ain't for her, man, she's a trooper, don't get me wrong, but she needs to be with one of those doctor-lawyer-type niggers I'm on the grind and all I can do is bring her down, ya feel me?" said Koran. "Let's eat, man, can I have the steak and eggs and a glass of grape juice? Yo, Dolla, get whatever you want, man."

"I'll take the same thing he's haven'."

"Yo, let me run something past you, I think that nigger Lil' L is the one who really tried to kill me."

"For what?"

"Shit and even more so, why?"

"So hold the fuck up," Dolla said, "you mean it was that Lil' L mother fucker who shot at you, but wasn't that nigger in jail?"

"That's the crazy shit," Koran said to Dolla, "when I saw him after he got out he was fucken' around and hit me right in the same place I got shot, but when I asked him who told him he said his sister told him when I hadn't seen her ass to tell her. I need to find that nigger Sha's bitch ass and see what he tells me, and if shit doesn't add up I have to stop his clock. So where the fuck is Lil' L? I need to find this nigger also," said Koran, "but damn, if I do something to Lil' L that might scare off Sha's ass, and that nigger is just as wrong for snitchen' to the police, what the fuck ever happened to death before dishonor?"

"That's some real shit right there, Koran."

"I see the game has changed and as for me this is where I get out," said Koran.

An hour passed when all of a sudden Koran's pager wen off and it was L, AKA Money.

"What's up, nigger?"

"Yo, what the fuck happened in the park, I drove past, I saw police all over that mother fucker."

"Ya boy Sha got caught and they ran up on me, leaving the park, they took my money and smacked me around a little, I got out on bail."

"That nigger was your boy, not mines."

"Where the fuck were you?" said Koran.

"I dipped into a motel and waited to see what was up."

"This nigger Sha has to go, man, need for you to find where he is and get back to me."

"I got you, man, I got you," said L.

"Hello, who is this?"

"I got some good news for you, nigger, I found where Sha lives."

"Good, for that nigger is as good as dead."

Later on that night, Lil' L and Koran met up.

"So you sure you want to do this?" said Lil' L, AKA Money.

"What kind of shit is that to ask? This nigger has brought me nothing but heat. So, Lil' L, are you down for this or what, after all you brought the nigger to me."

"He lives right there in that white house, I'll take front and you take the back," said Lil' L.

"You sure he's in there, L?"

"Yeah, nigger, I'm sure, Koran."

Koran told L to give him a minute, then ran to the back of the house to see if the house alarm was on and to kill the phone line. Lil' L waited and counted to ten, then went in the house. They found Sha and his girlfriend in the house.

"You ever been touched by God?" Koran yelled and put two in his head. Koran looked at Lil' L and gave him that look.

"You see what happens to snitches, bitch!" as Lil' L shot Sha twice in the chest. "What about her?"

"We got who we came for, let's go, nigger."

Lil' L and Koran dipped out the house and over a fence.

Lil' L said, "Yo, throw ya gun in the sewer."

"I got rid of my shit back there," Koran said as he waited for Lil' L to throw his shit away.

Standing there looking at Lil' L smiling, Koran thought about killing L, yet was wondering how could a person try to kill you and be the same person who just helped you kill somebody?

It was now a week before Koran would go to court, and him and Lil' L were watching TV. Koran noticed the reporter say something about an ice cream truck.

"Yo, what did they say on the news just now?"

"Some guy who owned a neighborhood ice cream truck or some shit was found dead not too far from his home."

Just then the tears from Koran's eyes felt heavy, for the only man he knew and loved was dead.

"What's wrong, man, did you know him? Hell, he was just a fucken' guy that drove an ice cream truck, nigger, get over it," said L.

"If it wasn't all these people sitting in here, I would blow his fucken' head off," said Koran to himself as he asked the bartender to pour him a double.

It was Sunday morning and Koran was pulling out the one suit he hated to wear.

"Damn, I can't believe Tommy's gone, it seems like I just saw him yesterday." Koran stood in front of his mirror, tying his tie as he got ready for Tommy's funeral. "Okay, I have my keys, my pager, my wallet, I know it's disrespectful to bring a gun to a funeral but after that week I been haven' I can't afford not to be strapped," Koran said to himself as he was about to walk out the door.

Koran pulled up to the funeral parlor and couldn't believe all the cars and people that were there. As he stepped out of his cab he noticed a lot of older heads like Rondu, Prince from Queens, and Black from South Side.

"Yo, peace," Koran said to Prince and Rondu. "Damn, I didn't know you guys knew Tommy."

"It's a small world, baby, when you get our age you come to learn it's better to be on the sideline rather than all in the limelight," said Prince. "So how's business?"

"And what business is that?" asked Koran.

"Come on, baby, ain't no need to be putting up a front here, look around you," said Rondu, "every man or woman you see owns something somewhere with their name on it, and they all came to pay their respects."

"I'm maintaining, you know, striven' to get that real money," said Koran.

"It's about that time to go inside," said one of the guys standing outside smoking a Newport.

An hour passed and everyone was starting to exit the funeral parlor.

"Yo, Koran! Hold up," said Rondu, "somebody wants to have a word with you."

Just then a guy walked up to him surrounded by six bodyguards. "So you're Koran? Damn, I thought you would be older, shit! You don't look even 25. Pardon me, I'm Tommy's brother Tiny. Walk with me. My brother would write me when I was in the Feds talking about you."

"He was a good man," said Koran. "If you don't mind me asken'," said Koran, "how was he killed?"

"All we know is whoever the person was killed him fucked up his place, I guess trying to find where the dope was," said Tiny, "as if my brother would be dumb enough to keep that shit in his home. Don't worry," said Tiny, "we'll find those niggers, if you happen to hear something let me know, here's my private number. If you need anything call me or our sister Kellie right here. Kellie! Come here for a minute. Koran, this is Kellie, this is Koran."

"How are you doing?" said Koran.

"You can call me Caramel. I could be better but this shit comes with the game," she said as she turned to Tiny and asked for a light. "The niggers who killed my brother will pay, you can believe that."

"How is it I never met any of you, yet you seem to know me?" asked Koran.

"I run shit out of state for my brother," said Caramel.

"I just heard my brother mention ya name a few times here and there, and as for me, youngen'," Tiny said, "the only way most people meet me is when they find me sitting in their living room."

"Do you need a ride somewhere?" said Caramel.

"Sure, if you could just drop me off on Jamaica Ave., that would be cool."

"Okay, that's my whip parked over there. Koran, I want you to call me sometimes, if you just want to talk," as she grabbed his hand and wrote down her number.

"Damn," Koran said to himself as she pulled off in her black BMW, "why couldn't I have met her before now? I know she has to be older than me, if she wasn't Tommy's sister I'd damn sure get with her sexy ass," as he walked into Dunkin' Donuts and got a cup of coffee.

Just then Koran got a page from his Uncle Steven.

"Shit! I wonder what he wants," said Koran. "Yo, Steve, what's up?"

"Nothing much, I just got out of church with your grandmother, I was just checken' on my favorite nephew and was seeing if you wanted to go to the Knicks game tonight?"

"Yo, that's cool, man, just let me know what time and I'm there."

"Well, let me get off ya grandmother's phone because you know how she gets, just be at my house about 6 o'clock."

It was about 9 P.M. and the game was over.

"Yo, Koran, let's go across the street and have a drink before you break out," said his Uncle Steven.

"Yo, man, I don't remember the last time I did some shit like this," Koran said.

"Yeah, I remember when ya ass was little, how you wanted to always leave the house with me and how I would take you with me to the movies on Fulton Street."

"Those were the days," said Koran.

"Now look at cha," said Steven. "You're ya own man, got ya own house and shit, yet you do know at some point or another all that fast money and shit comes to an end?"

"Yo, Steve, I hear what ya sayen', I'm just trying to come up, I don't see me being in the game when I'm 40, 50 years old."

"Well, ya ass ain't even 30 and from the looks of things you seem to be doing pretty good."

"Yo, man, I just want to save up enough money so I can have my own shit and not work for somebody, and I damn sure don't want to live the way I did coming up, no food, no hot water, rats and roaches, fuck that! I will never go back to being poor."

"Do you want to come back to my house?" said Steven. "You know your cousin would be happy to see you."

"Na, man, I have to get up early on Monday to go to court, I think I'm just going to call it a night."

Ring, ring, ring.

"Hello, Koran, it's me, Sweet P, I just called to wish you good luck in court and to let you know everything will be okay, I just want you to know I'm sorry things turned out this way."

"Yo need to forget about me, ain't no telling what's going to happen when I go to court. Ask yourself, do you really see yourself sticken' around if I have to do some time? I don't," said Koran. "Yo, my cab is here," then he hung up the phone.

It was now 9:30 A.M. and Koran was sitting in the hallway, waiting for his lawyer.

"How are you, Mr. Biggs? It seems like I have some good news and some bad news for you."

"Just tell me whatever you're going to tell me," said Koran.

"Well, it seems that the sudden death of a Mr. Tony Young, AKA Sha, the police don't have a case, the good news is the judge is about to order that you get three years on paper," said his lawyer.

"On paper, damn, man! Shit, I guess it's better than going to jail."

"You know, before the death of the person who they were saying worked for you, they were looking to turn this over to the Feds?" said Koran's lawyer.

"I remember you telling me that, and like I told them, I'm a fucken' solider and I ain't no snitch. So fuck the Feds and the police. Tommy did tell me that."

"We have to go in court, for it's about to start."

"We the court here by find Koran Biggs guilty and is to be sentenced to three years' probation. Mr. Biggs, it is the order of the court that you hereby be sentenced to three years' probation. I want you to know this, young man, if this wasn't your first arrest I'd throw the book at you. God is on your side, young man; this would be a good time for you to turn your life around and stop wasting your life away. Next case."

"Well, Mr. Biggs, my job is done here, what you do now is up to you, yet you have my number if I can be of some help."

"Thank you, Mr. Wolf, for all your help."

As Koran was walking out of the court building feeling happy to walk away with just probation, he ran into the cops who had been fucking with him since Shawn got killed.

"You must be one lucky mother fucker, Koran," said Officer Smith, "but you think about this, one way or another I will bust your ass and your friend, you watch."

"Yo, whatever, I'll be holding court in the fucken' street before your bitch ass arrests me," Koran said, then walked out the court building and jumped into a cab.

"Where to, sir?"

"Flushing Queens, I'll give you the address, just drive."

During the ride in the cab, Koran started to think about how he needed to make his life right and get out the game, yet in the back of his mind he felt he could not let Lil' L live after not just for maybe haven' somebody try to kill him, but for maybe killing the only father Koran ever really had, even if he was an ice cream driver who pushed dope.

Ring, ring, ring.

"Yo, who is this?" said Lil' L.

"Yo, nigger, it's Koran!"

"What's up, man?" said Lil' L.

"Yo, I got hit with three-year probation," Koran told Lil' L.

"Damn, nigger, that's all?"

"Nigger, you sound as if you were expecting more," Koran said. "Well, I'm sorry to disappoint you. Look, man, I'm out, from here on out do your thing."

"Nigger, what is this shit you're talking about?" said Lil' L. "We in this shit for the long ride, Koran, ain't no getten' out."

"Pardon me, look, nigger, let me spell it out, I'M OUT! You can have all this shit," said Koran.

"I give you a week, a month at the most, before you be jumpen' on my dick," said Lil' L. "This is about you just wanting to leave me for that bitch you been fucken'; see where that bitch be when the money runs out!" said Lil' L.

"You out of line, nigger," said Koran.

"I know all about her fat ass, she is only with your ass for your money," said Lil' L."

"Yo, I gots to go. You sound real gay right with this leave you, shit, L, I'm a grown-ass man."

Koran was sitting in his living room home and he was starting to think about the conversation him and Lil' L had more and more and was starting to feel like Lil' L would not let him get out the game without doing something. An hour later Koran got a call from Dolla, who told him that the house Koran used to live in was shot up earlier today and the police had shit taped off and to just be careful also, some niggers named Dave and Kevin or Sam and Dave had been riding around asking about him, for they pushed up on his little brother asking him if he knew somebody named Koran.

Koran hung up the phone, then Dolla then checked on his grandmother to make sure shit was okay, told his grandmother he was going to come by there in about an hour.

"Shit, I need to call Sweet P because if niggers are over where Dolla lives asking people about me, then they probably know where Sweet P lives. Yo, Sweet P, this is Koran, is ya mom's boyfriend Rusty there?"

"He just walked in the house, why, do you need to speak to him?" she said.

"Look, I don't have time for this shit right now, can you give him the phone?"

"Yo, Koran, what's up, man?"

"Yo, can you talk?"

"I'm good, man, what's up?"

"Yo, the nigger I ran with I think just had some nigger shoot up my house out in Rosedale, and it's two niggers over by you asking people if they seen me."

"So nigger, what's ya next move?" said Rusty.

"I have to get this nigger before he gets me, right now I need to run to my grandmother's real quick to make sure shit is okay over there, I'll be by your house in about 20 minutes, my cab is outside," and hung up the phone.

Koran put on his vest and grabbed a few clips and his gun, then ran out the door.

"Yo, what's up?" said the cabdriver.

"Shit is hot right now, yo have anybody on 228th been asking about me?"

"Na, man, not that I know of," said the cab driver.

"Yo, we're going to need to make a few stops and if I tell you to run a fucken' light I mean run the fucken' light," said Koran.

"What, you got beef, man?"

"Just drive, first stop I need for you to swing past baby girl's house; when you get there drive around the block one time and park on the next block and wait."

A few minutes passed and the cab was now on Farmers as Koran made sure his shit was off safety.

"Okay, now pull up there on the corner of 115th. This is cool right here, yo, if you hear, see anything, hit me on the hip."

Knock, knock, knock. It was Koran at the back door of where Sweet P lived.

"Yo, Rusty, man, you still got that M11 I gave you?"

"Oh, nigger, I love that shit, yeah, and I got a new AK-47."

"Now these niggers that are looking for me, I know them, they're Lil' L's cousins or some shit, we did some shit out of state a few times, they like to use hammers and shit, now I'm not sure if they're going to come here, just want to make sure all of you are okay. I don't want none of my shit coming to your doorstep for some shit I'm into," said Koran. "Me and baby girl ain't together anymore but nevertheless, I need to know all of you are safe."

"You know how I get down, kid. Go handle ya business, I got this over here. Look, nigger, you know you're always welcome here, I can't say that for some of these other niggers that girl insists on dating, I got something for their ass if they come here," said Rusty.

"Yo, my ride is waiting."

Koran jumped the gate to the back of the house, then spotted his cab but also noticed a tan car parked on the corner.

"Let me think for a minute," said Koran, "I need to make sure that's them, and if that is them I need to kill them before I go to my grand-mother's house."

Koran ran to a payphone on the corner and told his cabdriver to drive past the tan car to drive around the block, he told the cabdriver, "If that's them, when you move they might follow me and to pick me up on 116th by the store on the corner."

Koran waited up the street as he watched his cabdriver drive away, and a minute or so later so did that tan car.

"If I can only catch them niggers without them seeing me," Koran said to himself as he walked up behind the car, trying to get a good look. "Damn, that's Sam right there, now where the fuck is Dave? For if you see one, then the other one is not that far behind."

Koran pulled out his gun and walked up alongside the tan car, shooting the driver in the head twice, then out the corner of his eye he saw Dave coming behind him with a hammer as he shot Dave in the chest and got hit in the ribs by Dave's hammer.

"Just like a nigger to bring a hammer to a gunfight, ya fucken' cousin couldn't just leave me alone, he had to try and kill a nigger."

"Money wants you dead," said Dave, "with you around you will always be a threat to him."

That was all the information Koran needed to hear. His last words to Dave were "Have you ever been touched by God?" and he shot Dave in the head.

"Yo, mother fucker, let's go," said the cabdriver.

Koran took one last look at Dave and saw a watch he knew too well; it was the watch he gave Tommy for his last birthday.

"Change of plans, man, just get me to Jamaica Ave., from there you go your way and I go mine. Yo, take this money and if anybody asks your ass was in Atlantic City gambling," said Koran.

"Yo, Koran, man, you sure about that?" said the cabdriver.

"It's safe this way, if anybody is looking they can't tie us as being together, let me out right here," said Koran.

Koran waited 'til the cabdriver pulled off, then ran up the block to Parsons and jumped on the train.

"I know it will not be long before Lil' L finds out that his cousins are dead."

Just then Koran got a 911 page from Sweet P.

"Shit, she will have to wait until I get off the train at Broadway Junction to catch the A Train," said Koran.

A few more stops and Koran got off the train.

"I need a damn phone," Koran said to himself, running from the J Train to the A Train. "Yo, hello," said Koran.

"Yo, this is Rusty, man, you need to talk to Sweet P, hold on."

"Koran, where are you?" said Sweet P.

"Right now it's better you don't know that, are all of you okay?" said Koran.

"Yeah, we're okay, we all heard a lot of shooting and they have everything taped off."

"Yo, I have to go," and just as Koran was about to hang up the phone he noticed he had some blood on his clothes. "Damn, I need to make it to my grandmother's without anybody noticing me," as he walked down the stairs and saw his train coming.

Koran took the train to Grant Avenue, there he walks through the park and up the back stairs to his grandmother's.

Ring, ring, ring.

"Hello?" said his grandmother.

"It's your grandson, Koran."

"My grandson?"

"Yes, your grandson." Koran then opened the door.

"Do you want something to eat?" she asked.

"I'm okay, can I use your bathroom?" Koran said.

"As long as it's not my phone, and make sure you use the hand towels on the back of the door."

Koran went in the bathroom and closed the door, pulled off his shirt, and noticed it looked like a few of his ribs might be broken.

"I'm going to fix this the best I can, hang around for a couple of hours, then get the hell out of here and go find this nigger L."

"Do you still have some of my clothes here?"

"They should be in the hallway closet, why do you need to change your clothes?" she asked.

"I spilled something on my jeans," Koran said.

"So have you spoken to your mother?"

"No, Peaches, and for what?" Koran said. "You know, for a long time I used to walk around feeling like I was out of place, my mother running around in the street, my father acting like he doesn't have a son, and me just getting moved from this person's house to the next. I don't have shit to say to her."

"Look, you watch your damn mouth in my house! I'm still your grandmother and she is still your mother, her ass was fifteen when she had you running the streets and smoken' that shit. Everybody makes mistakes," said his grandmother, "you just have to know how to forgive. I understand what you're saying, but do you hear what I'm saying?"

"I hear you, I hear you, Peach, yet some things just can't be fixed or a person can forget, do you know what it's like for a child to have to fight just about every man that comes in your home as they treat you like dirt, then smile in your face? She made me feel like I wasn't important, for she always put some nigger in the street before me and that is something when I have kids I will never do. When she brought home Chuck, me and him would fight not just with words but physically, that shit didn't matter to her. With Marc the same damn thing; I became my so-called mother's doormat for the niggers she came home with."

"You need to let go of all that hate, Koran. Jesus and I love you."

"I know you do, as for Jesus he's no different than my father, never around but wants all the glory. I'm this way because my so-called parents made me this way!"

"Well, I'm going in the back to lay down, you make sure you lock my door when you leave," said Peaches. "I'll let you know when I'm leaving."

"Damn, I'm bugging the fuck out," said Koran to himself. "That nigger doesn't even know where my grandmother lives. Can I have a drink, Peaches?"

"Just don't drink all my good shit," she said, then asked Koran, "when are you going to church with me? Boy, I want you to remember this, you live by the sword, you die by the sword, and if you're not staying here then I'm going to bed."

"I'm leaving right after I finish this drink," Koran said, then left. "Shit, I need something stronger than that fucken' drink, that nigger got me good with that fucken' hammer," Koran said as he looked in his pocket to see if he had a mess tab. "Shit, I need two but one will do for now," as he popped the mess tab and checked to see how many clips he had. "Too late to go back to my grandmother's house, I could have checked my safe in my old room. If I could make it to my house, I could make a few calls and see what's going on out on the street."

Koran deeped through a few apartment buildings until he found himself on Knew Lots Ave. at a cabstand.

"Yo, is car #25 here?"

"Yo, Koran."

"What's up, Pa?"

"Just trying to live, man, yo, this is the address, I just need to rest my eyes for a minute," said Koran and went to sleep in the backseat.

Twenty minutes later, out in Flushing Queens, "Yo, Pa Pa!"

"Yo, Koran, we're here."

"Yo, Elijah, help me in my house," said Koran.

"Damn, Pa Pa, you don't look so good."

"Yo, Elijah, do you have anything on you?"

"For you, Pa Pa, the best fish scale on this side of Brooklyn."

"Good looken' out," said Koran as he slid Elijah 100 dollars and said to close his door on the way out and not to worry about his dog.

"Those mother fuckers always did have the best coke," as Koran laughed, knowing that the same person who just gave him some coke over a year ago, him and L beat for a half a key by giving his boy all singles and his dumb ass didn't count it.

Koran sat in the chair, took a hit a coke, and put his head back and closed his eyes. It was now after 12 and Koran was woken by his dog barken'.

"What's wrong, boy?" as Koran grabbed his gun and looked around.

After realizing it was nothing, he opened his back door and let his dog out, changed the bandages on his ribs, and looked for something to wear.

"I need to go by L's dad's house and see if I see his car there, then put some hot shit in his ass."

It was now 12:40 A.M., and Koran just reached Lil' L's parents' house.

If I'm lucky, I'll catch his ass over there, Koran thought, *if not I'll snatch his fucken' sister at school;*

her ass will tell me where he is.

"Yo, drive around the block one more time," Koran told the cabdriver. "Fuck it, let's go," Koran said, "I don't see who I'm looking for, take me home and wake me up when you get there, okay?"

It was Friday morning, and Koran knew he needed to get his ass up and out to Queens if he wanted to catch Lil' L's sister Stacey before school started.

So he got up, let his dog out, and looked for something to wear. "Damn, can't believe I'm up this time of the morning," Koran said as he headed to the shower.

Twenty minutes later Koran was out the shower and was preparing to get dressed, with no time to lose he let his dog back in the house as he told himself, "Fuck it, I'll grab something to eat when I get out there."

Not wanting to use the cabdriver that he always took after using him in the getaway of the murder of Sam and Dave, Koran called a local cab from off of Parsons Blvd. to pick him up a few blocks from where he lived.

"A, Mister. How long are we going to wait out here?" the driver asked.

"As long as I need you to wait." Koran saw Stacey getting off the school bus and handed the cabdriver $50 and told him to wait.

"Hey, Stacey," Koran said as he crossed the street. "Have you seen your brother? What's a matter, Stacey, you look like you seen a ghost?"

"My brother is going to kick your ass," she said as she walked towards the school door.

"Trick, please you tell your brother all I wanted was out but he didn't want that, so he tried to have me killed. You let your brother know never send a boy to do a man's job, tell your brother to meet me at Brookfield Park tonight at midnight and we can settle this once and for all. Oh, and by the way, Stacey, if I wanted to harm you, ya ass would be in a body bag right now, you remember to tell his ass what I said, midnight Brookfield Park."

Just then a security guard came over to where Stacey and Koran were asking Stacey if there was any problem.

"There's no problem, so why don't you take your rent-a-cop ass back over there before I make you famous," said Koran.

Not wanting to go home and not having anywhere to go, Koran went to the McDonald's up the street from Stacey's school to eat breakfast.

"Hey, Koran, is that you? What are you doing around here?" a voice said as Koran got his food and was about to sit down.

"You know, it's funny I ran into you, I ran into your friend Lil' L the other night at a club, where I work part time at."

"Hey, Sharon, how have you been?"

"I'm okay, just working hard, about to drop off my son at my mother's house before I go to my other job at Sunrise, you need to stop by sometimes. Here's my number, call me or come by the club; you know where Manhattan Proper is, right?"

"Yeah, I know the place," as he finished his food.

Koran took Sharon's number and told her to take care as he got up to empty his tray. "At one time I may have wanted to hit that, but ain't no telling how many dicks this mud kicker had since we last saw each other. Females are funny," Koran said to himself. "When I was broke her ass didn't have the time for a nigger, now I'm maken' money, she wasn't to give me some ass, fuck her," as he walked out of McDonald's heading towards a payphone on the corner.

"Well, if it ain't my favorite Little Criminal, Mr. Koran Biggs," an officer said, as another cops sat on the side of the police car eating a jelly donut and drinking coffee.

"What the hell you want," said Koran, "don't you have something to do other than always fucken' with me?"

"A few days ago two people over on 115 and Farmers were killed, you wouldn't happen to know anything about that now?"

"Why would I?" said Koran.

"Look, mother fucker," said the officer as he threw his coffee and donut on the ground, "that shit has your name all over it!"

"You got witness or a murder weapon?" said Koran. "If not get the fuck out my face!"

"Look, you little fucken' punk, me and my partner here can easily just grab your black ass and put two in your fucken' head and nobody wouldn't even miss you. Do us both a favor and get the fuck out of Queens, even better get the hell out of New York."

As the officers were getting in their car, the one who killed Shawn said, "One more thing, tough guy, when you got shot over there on 228th what name popped in your head? What, you think we didn't know about that?" and pulled off.

"What the fuck is it with these two cops? Why the fuck does it seems like everywhere I go they fucken' pop up? And how is it that they know about me getting shot? Shit! I kill these two mother fuckers and the whole police station will be looking for my ass, I need to find a way to get them off my ass. Damn, is it because Tommy is dead? Okay, nigger, you're thinking too much, stay focused.

"I remember a time when I knew nothing about killing, nor did I want to kill anyone, now it seems like it's the only way for me to find peace, for I hate this life I live. On one hand I can buy anything I want, then on the other every time I go somewhere I have to be wondering if the cops are going to fuck with me or if I run into somebody that I got beef with; I just want a normal life, yet the hand that I have been dealt seems to only show me if I want out, then it will mean all the way out and that fucken' means killing L before he kills me."

Koran flagged a cab down.

"Where to, sir?"

"Flushing Queens, you can drop me off by Queens College."

It was now about noon and Koran told the cabdriver to let him out on the corner and to keep the change. Koran started to question himself as to what went wrong. How could two friends who at one point were like brothers now be out to kill each other?

Just then Koran's phone rang.

"Hello?"

"Yeah, nigger, this is Lil' L, I understand you sent a message to me saying meet you at Brookfield Park? Yo, if you ever come near my sister again—"

"Cut the small talk," said Koran, "it wasn't me who started all of this, all I wanted was to make money and get out of NY. I never knew greed would make a mother fuck flip like that. I loved you like a brother and in return you try and have me killed, not once but twice."

"You know how the game is," Lil' L said and hung up the phone.

"Damn, he didn't even try denying the shit."

Bam, then it hit him. Sharon said about seeing L at the club and figured that would be the perfect place to hit him at, and the hell with meeting at the park, yet he would need a little help in pulling that off and he knew of the perfect person: Tommy's sister Caramel.

"Now what the hell did I do with that number, 740-7******."

Ring, ring, ring.

"Yes, hello!"

"May I speak to Caramel, please, this is Koran."

"Well, hello, this is Caramel; I was just about to get in the bathtub, hold on, please. Okay, I'm back, so how are you?"

"I'm okay," said Koran.

"It's funny that you would call me now, I was starting to think you weren't going to call."

"I've been meaning to call, I've just been ripped and running taking care of a few things."

"So is this business or pleasure? And please tell me it's pleasure." She waited for Koran to answer, and before he could Caramel said to him, "Do you know where the IHOP on Hill Side is?"

"I've been there before," Koran said.

"Meet me there in one hour and please, baby, don't be late."

Koran, unlike those who he used to be with, never had a problem with sleeping with someone who he was friends with or who was in the same business they were in, yet Koran knew there was a big chance that seeing her may lead to more than just talk and mixing pleasure with business was dangerous. Yet he needed her help and in the back of his mind he wanted to see her as well.

"Shit, I have enough time to walk my dog, change clothes, and meet with her sexy ass."

At this point things with him and Sweet P were pretty much over, too much had happened between them for him to be feeling like he would be cheating on her if he did sleep with Caramel.

It was about ten minutes to one as Koran pulled up in front of IHOP, and he found Caramel sitting in a booth in the back, looking thicker than a Snickers. Koran had been with older women before but this time things were different, yet in the back of his mind he knew it could be nothing more than a good fuck because she was Tommy's sister and he wanted out of the lifestyle in which she lived.

"How are you, Caramel?" Koran said.

"Nice seeing you, Koran," as she kissed him on the cheek. "Well, I'll get right down to the reason I asked to meet you here," Caramel said. "It should be obvious that I'm attracted to you, and from the vibe I was getting when we first met you felt the same way."

"Damn!" Koran said. "Please understand, you are Tommy's sister."

"And your point is what?" Caramel said. "We're both adults."

"Tommy was like a father to me, and in some ways I would be disrespecting him by getting with you, plus in the back of my mind I'm wondering why.

"Look, Koran, I loved my brother as a sister would love her brother, yet as a woman my brother has nothing to do with you and me, don't get it twisted, when my brother would mention you, you were going to be nothing more than a quick fuck, but then when I saw you and we got to talking it was something about you that had me feeling like you're the one."

Just then a waitress came and asked to take their order. Koran ordered the steak and eggs.

"Make that two," Caramel said.

"Yo, might as well know, last week I ran into a little trouble, two guys tried to kill me over on 116th and Farmers, come to find out the same person who sent them was the same person who killed your brother," said Koran.

"How do you know this?" asked Caramel.

"I know this because before I blew his brains all over the sidewalk, he told me, plus he had on the watch I gave Tommy. I ran into a girl we both knew who told me that he's been going to this club called Manhattan Proper, where she works at a lot, so I figured that would be a good place as any to get his ass," said Koran.

"I need a fucken' blunt after the shit you just hit me with, Koran. Oh, and back to you and me, you know we're only a few years apart? What, you seeing somebody?"

"No, I'm single."

"Good answer," Caramel said.

"Looks like our food is here, because I'm starving," said Koran.

"I noticed each time I saw you, you're always getting out of a cab, one of things your brother taught me was never let them see you coming, so in a cab I blend in more."

"It makes sense," Caramel replied.

"Look at you in ya BMW."

"Oh, you like that?"

"Can't lie, it was hot."

Caramel laughed and said, "That's just what my brother said when he brought it."

"Wait, Tommy bought you that BMW?"

"No, he bought it for you, he wanted it to be a surprise, I'm more of a truck kind of chick, more like when I drive move out my way.... I could see you now just floating in that BMW."

"I'm ready for that blunt now, what's up?"

"I want to be there when he dies," said Caramel.

"I will do better than that," Koran said. "I'll give you his fucken' head on a platter."

"I will need for you to go to the club with me, Koran. So how will we even know he will be there?" said Caramel.

"Well, from what this chick was saying he's there all the time, I have a picture of him at my house, just need for you to push up on him and I'll be right outside, you take him to a motel where I'll get a room at and we put his ass to sleep."

"Sounds like a plan, I see you thought of just about everything."

"For what this mother fucker did to my brother, he has to die," said Caramel.

"Damn, this is some good-ass weed," Koran said as she passed him the blunt.

"So let me ask you something, Koran. How did you get mixed up with him?"

"When we were younger it was me, him, a cat named Shawn, and Randy, we did B. N.E.s, then when crack came we got into the drug game, we were all close, then when shit like greed came into the picture, I guess Lil' L just didn't see shit the same and figured it's better to have me killed and keep it all rather than to allow me to have what's mine. Shit, he tried two times to kill me, he always wanted to be the next Neno Brown, as for me I'm just striven' to live," said Koran.

"Koran, in this game some of the craziest shit happens, you just need to know when to get in and when to get out, for none of this shit last forever."

Well, it was about an hour later and Koran and Caramel just hit New Jersey."

"So where are we going?" said Koran.

Caramel looked at him and said, "My house," as she turned in a driveway waiting for the gate to open."

"Damn, you live out here? This is some real nice shit," said Koran.

"Just because you come from the projects doesn't mean you have to stay there," said Caramel. "I know so many cats in the game who are either dead, in jail, or hooked on the same shit they started pushing, as for me, Koran—"

"Caramel, I just want to be able to open my refrigerator and not see the back of it, not have bills and not know how to pay them, but most of all when I have children I don't want them to ever have a need in the world, most of all do the shit I did as a lil' shorty comen' up. Oh, and I see me owning my own company."

"Baby, look," said Caramel, "it's a hustle; some people are born to be leaders and other followers. You street smart, I'm book smart, yet we're both after the same thing, if it wasn't for me the Feds would have taken all of my brother's shit; you and my brother were close, so I can tell you these things. After Tommy got knocked a few times, I took my ass to college and got my degree, the fucken' jails are full of brothers and sisters in there who if only they would have thought more carefully things would have turned out different. You and I both have done our share of dirt, yet those mother fuckers in the White House, now they're the ones who are pimpen' everybody; these little niggers nowadays get money and they think they're the shit.

"I see now why my brother took a liking to you the way he did, the nigger who killed my brother killed the wrong one. Tommy went legit years ago, it's his name and who he was that had so many cats wanting to be like a lot of other dead brothers out here; truth be told it's my other brothers who run shit, they wanted that life and wasn't about to get a 9-5, so Tommy said they could have that shit. I asked you to meet up with me on Hill Side for most of those stores and a few homes over there Tommy owned, now it's his not-so-little sister has to put her shit on hold to take care of that."

"Damn," said Koran, "now I see why he was always talking to me, trying to pull my coat, I remember the last time I spoke to him, he was talking to me as if he was trying to tell me to get out this shit, and after we take care of Lil' L's ass I'm going to do just that...get the fuck out of New York!"

"So where will you go?" asked Caramel.

"Who knows, Ohio seems like a good place for me to start my life over," said Koran.

"Have a seat and I'll be right back, the bar is over there."

About 10 or 15 minutes later Caramel came back and sat on the couch across from Koran and said, "What's wrong, you're not used to seeing me not wearing what I had on earlier?"

"It's not that at all, I just find you to be a very beautiful woman."

At that moment Koran got up and sat next to Caramel.

"Don't worry, baby, I don't bite," said Caramel, "only if you want me to."

Caramel reached over to kiss Koran and said, "Is that a gun in your jeans or are you that excited to see me?"

"This is all me, love," and pulled out his nine and said, "Now this is my gun," as Koran put his hand on Caramel's face and gently kissed her lips. "I've been wanting to do that ever since I last saw you."

"Well, now is your chance," Caramel said, "and a lot more," as she leaned back on her white leather couch.

Koran started to think for a minute that if he slept with her, if it was wrong he didn't want to be right.

A few hours passed and they both found themselves lying in Caramel's bed with both their clothes making a trail all the way to the bed.

Just then Koran got a phone call. "Hello?"

"Yo, Koran, it's me, Goldie, I'm at the airport."

"Yo, what's up, man, I'll be there as soon as I can, what airport are you at? Okay, JFK, be there soon. A baby, I need to run to the airport and pick up a friend of mine, I'm going to need for you to meet with me around 11:30 P.M. on Jamaica Ave. by the Persons Train Station. I'll give you the picture of L then."

Caramel said, "The keys to the Beamer are over there, it's yours anyway," as she rolled over and went to sleep.

"Keep it warm, keep it tight, baby, I'll talk to you later," he said as he headed for her bedroom door.

"Goldie, sorry about haven' you wait here so long."

"Jump in. Yo, man, why didn't you call me sooner?" said Goldie.

"Come on, you and I have never been one to have somebody else handle our shit," said Koran. "I need to get close to this nigger and that's why I called you, plus it maybe a few niggers with him."

"Cool, man, it's fine with me," said Goldie. "I'm going to drop you off at the motel then."

"Call you when I want you to leave, I need for you to get to the Manhattan Proper early so you can see who comes and goes," said Koran.

"I got it, man, I still think you don't have to be there, I could kill this nigger and whoever else he's with and be up the street haven' a Coke before the police even get there," said Goldie.

"Na, man, I need to be there, this bitch-ass nigger tried more than once to have me killed, now I'm going to show him how us Brooklyn cats get down. Here's the room key, it's room 419, call me if ya need anything."

Koran realized he left Caramel's house before he had a chance to take a shower, for the smell of her bath and body wash was all in Koran's clothes. "I broke a major rule sleeping with her today," Koran said to himself, "but damn, did she look good in those boy shorts."

Koran parked Caramel's car around the corner from where he lived and slid in the back of his house, where he was greeted by his dog, Prince.

"Hey, boy, I sure would hate for somebody to come in this house." Koran thought, scratching his head as he let his dog outside. "Being with a woman is cool but smelling like one I can do without," as Koran went to take a shower.

It was now 10:30 P.M. and it was time for Koran to get up and get ready, for right about now nothing could go wrong.

Ring, ring, ring.

"Yo, Koran, this is Goldie, I'm just about ready, I just need to fix my wig and I'll see you there; I'll let you know if he shows up before you get there."

"I'm getting ready now. Yo, Goldie, how will I know where you are in there?" asked Koran.

"I'll find you." Goldie then hung up the phone.

With everything in play, Koran just needed to make one call and that was to Caramel.

"Baby, don't forget, 11:30 P.M."

"I'm just about ready to leave, I'll see you soon."

It was a good night to wear black, Koran thought. *Fuck it, I'm only going to Manhattan Proper. Can't believe he goes to that hole in the wall. Shit, it's almost time for me to go, just need to grab my gun and the car keys, then I'm out.*

It was now about 11:15 P.M. and Koran was waiting for Caramel, a few minutes passed and he saw a navy blue Benz pull up.

"Here's the picture of what Lil' L looks like," said Koran. "Goldie is inside already, try to hang around the bar, you will know when you see him," Koran told her. "He will be trying to show off, if we can hit him in the bathroom, cool, if not then we do what has to be done."

"Yo, man, the mother fucker is here and what looks like six deep."

"I'm on my way," said Koran. "Whatever you do, don't let that nigger leave! Damn, who would have thought this play would be so packed? This will make it easier for me to just slide in, came too far to turn back now."

Caramel parked her car and went in, she got a drink and began to look around for L. "It shouldn't be too hard to find him," she said to herself, with a lil' number like this on, shit, Stevie Wonder would notice her.

As she made her way to the bar she ordered a drink and checked to make sure her 380 was off safety that she had strapped to her thigh. Just think, Goldie was right by her and she didn't even noticed that was a man, not woman.

Koran walked in and started to look around, checking for an exit just in case shit got hot he had a way to get out. Koran was on his way to the bar when what looked like a girl said to him, "Koran, this is Goldie, they're over there in the bake, meet me over by that payphone so we can talk."

Koran went to the bar and ordered a drink. He saw Caramel by the bar so he told her, "Hey, baby, Lil' L and them are over there in the back; I'm on my way to the payphone to talk to Goldie."

Caramel looked to her left and said, "Koran, but the only person over there is that girl."

"That's no girl, Caramel, that's fucken' Goldie, he has been dressing like that since I known him, trust me, when shit gets thick everybody in here will find out he ain't fucken' playen'," said Koran. "Wait a few minutes, then see if you can sit somewhere not too far from him so you can catch his eye."

Caramel said, "Baby, I got this, I'm a woman, we know how to attract a man's attention," as she walked away.

Koran headed for the payphone to speak to Goldie. "Yo, what's up?" said Koran.

"We don't have all night," said Goldie, "the nigger been here since I called you, not sure when he might want to leave so if we're going to make a move we need to do it soon."

"Look," Koran said, "you see that brown-skin chick right there? I came with her, whatever you do and whoever you get to killing in this mother fucker don't kill her, plus she's going to help us."

"Help us, help us how?"

"She's going to get Lil' L away from those niggers and that's where you and I come in, trust me, ain't none of them niggers walking out of here," said Koran.

Caramel found the perfect table where Lil' L was more than sure to see her, on the other side of the club Goldie started to make his move, with Goldie on one side, Caramel on the other, and Koran in the middle, it seemed like the perfect plan.

In the back of the club, Lil' L and his crew were drinking bottles of Moët and smoking weed when Lil' L noticed Caramel.

"Yo, L," one of his boys said as he picked up a bottle of Moët. "Damn, they got some bitches up in here tonight, I'm fucken' something up in here," and laughed.

"That's your problem, y'all niggers are always talken', but never doing shit. Now you see girl over there, I'm about to leave you niggers and go get me some ass."

"Yo, yo, Money, what about that shit with Koran?" one of his boy said.

"Fuck Koran, that nigger, we will meet with him at 12, the next time we see that nigger his ass is mine, now leave me the fuck alone so I can go talk to shorty." Lil' L walked over to Caramel's table with a bottle of Moët in his hand. "Hey, baby, how you doing? My name is Money, what's yours, shorty?"

Caramel was heated like a mother fucker, for the person who had killed her brother was standing right in front of her, plus this punk who thought he was the king of New York had just called her shorty, as she said to herself, "I should shoot his ass right here, then it will be me needing a lawyer."

"My name is Karen, what did you say your name was?"

L sat down looking at Caramel's thick thighs and big breasts, smiled, and then looked over where his boys were and said to himself, "Boy, I can't wait to get up in that ass." L had no idea that the person he had been trying to kill was only a few feet away from him as Koran was just waiting for the right time to make his move.

At that moment one of Lil' L's boys noticed Goldie and headed to his table. "A yo, what's your name, sexy?" he said as he stood there smoking a blunt.

"My name is Kandy," said Goldie, "and what's yours?"

"I'm Bobby, a yo, me and my boys were just up in here chillen' and I notice how fine you look."

This nigger must be blind, high, or fucken' dumb, Goldie thought, *for he has no idea I'm not a woman, but that's just how I like these weak niggers to be, it makes it easier for me to put some hot shit it in their ass.*

Another one of Lil L's boys walked over to where Caramel and him were sitting and said, "Yo, L, are you sure about the thing with Koran, because it's getting late?"

"Look, right now I'm trying to talk to shorty, you niggers can do what you want."

Caramel then said, "It's getting late, maybe some other time."

"Hold on," Lil' L said and said to his boys, "I don't know about y'all niggers but I'm fucken' shorty tonight because if Bobby over there can pull a bitch I know I'm getting some pussy," then he said, "I'll get with you guys later."

Lil' L then came back to Caramel's table and said, "Yo, shorty, let's get the fuck out of here."

"This is perfect," Caramel said to herself as she was getting up; his dumb ass had pussy on the brain and thinking like that was what was going to get him killed.

Over on the other side of the club, Goldie saw Lil' L and Caramel leaving and waited for Koran to give him a signal as to what to do next.

A few minutes passed and Lil' L and Caramel had left the club, now it was only Koran, Goldie, and the six guys that came there with Lil' L.

Goldie then said to the guy he was talking to, "So Bobby, what's up with you and your friends over there?" as Koran was making his way to make sure Lil' L didn't get too far.

Back at the table where Lil' L's boys were, one of them got up to go to the bathroom and noticed Koran, then pulled out a gun. Bobby turned to see what was going on and found the last thing he saw was the flash of light from Goldie's gun as he took one to the face.

"Yo, that's that nigger right there, that's fucken' Koran."

Koran dipped behind a table he knocked over and started shooting, catching one of Lil' L's boys in the throat and another in the stomach and shoulder. With three guys left, Koran and Goldie made their move as another one of Lil' L's boys tried to get off a shot, catching Koran in the leg and once in the stomach before he was gunned down by Goldie.

At this time Caramel and Lil' L were sitting in Lil' L's car as Caramel told him to unzip his jeans, Lil' L heard that and did just that as he leaned his head back.

Back at the club people were running everywhere, trying hard not to get shot.

Koran yelled to Goldie, "Would you stop playen' with these niggers? I need to get the fuck out of here and find L!"

"Fuck you," yelled Goldie, "I got this, go find his ass!"

Koran headed for the door but before leaving he came head on with one of the bouncers who were on his way in, , Koran had to shoot his way out as Koran got outside and tried to see if he could see Caramel and Lil' L and headed toward the parking lot.

Caramel closed in to make her move as the people in the club started to run out, not sure if she should see what was going on, she decided to stay as Lil' L was sitting there with his eyes closed and pussy on his mind, not being able to see what was going on.

Caramel whispered in his ear, "Enjoy it, baby," as she leaned to kiss him on his neck, then cut Lil' L's throat with the razor she had in her mouth. "This is for my brother you killed, may you rot in hell," she said as she got out of his car.

Koran found Caramel getting out and started to hear police sirens, then said to Koran, "Oh, shit, you've been hit."

"Just get out of here," said Koran, "before the cops get here."

"What about you and Goldie?" Caramel yelled.

"Trust me, me and Goldie will be okay, and as for me this would be a damn good time to get the fuck out of New York, if you're ever in Ohio look me up," as he drove off down a dark street....

A few weeks went by and Koran got a call.

"Hey, sexy, this is Caramel, see, you're a hard man to keep up with, I see when you get ghost you really get ghost."

"Hey, beautiful," Koran said.

"There's a package on your doorstep, in it you will find something I'm sure you would want to know; after you do call me at the number in the envelope."

Koran opeed his door and found an envelope addressed to him, in the envelope there was a letter and a picture of someone Koran was with at one time.

The letter enclosed read: "Hey, fat head, by the time you get this letter I will have found this person who I understand some years back caused you a lot of pain, before you look at the photo I'm very aware that they went as far as sending a letter to the DEA, tipping them off about the guns you were running with my brother."

"This bitch in my eyes shitted on you, then bounced, but I found her ass," said Caramel. "I believe the chick's name was Veronica."

Koran looked at the photo and noticed what at one time looked like someone he once knew was now chopped up into little pieces, attached was a note that read: "This bitch wanted to run her fucken' mouth to the DEA, trying to get you sent back to prison, I'd kill a rock over you; this bitch had it coming, she had it coming, here's a first-class ticket to VA, come fuck with a real bitch. Criminals for Life," signed Kellie, AKA Caramel.